DICKENS
The
Socially Mobile Cat

DICKENS
The
Socially Mobile Cat

A. John Bird

Illustrated by
Douglas Hall

Eyebrow Illustrated Editions

First published in Great Britain 1991 by
Eyebrow Illustrated Editions
82 Sinclair Road London W14 0NJ

Copyright © Text A. John Bird 1991
© Illustrations Douglas Hall 1991

ISBN 1 872648 01 0

Filmset by First Typesetting & Design Limited
Catherine Wheel Road Brentford Middlesex

Printed by Butler & Tanner Limited
Frome Somerset

To

Pat Bird

CONTENTS

1

Acceptance
at
Last

On this, a warm spring afternoon, Dickens sat opposite the family house in Periodic Square observing a winged circus of sparrows and starlings warring over the undigested seeds hidden in the square's plenteous horsedroppings. Soon a man with a shovel and handcart would arrive and clear away the offending matter, but for the moment Nature's beaked scavengers were having a field day in the otherwise somnolent white stucco'd square. Although the birds appeared tantalizingly near, they were not near enough for Dickens to take one of their number without a sudden surge of energy, something that he seemed unprepared to commit. So he sat on the pavement in the shade of a great plane tree and watched, nonchalantly, expecting nothing from life and giving nothing in return.

This was the level of Dickens' inertia until he noticed a small, plump woman halt in front of No. 17. In itself, this was of little import to Dickens, lolling semi-recumbent opposite. If the arrival of the plump woman outside the family residence caused any passing attraction, it was probably due to the strangeness of the woman's hat, which had all the appearance of comprising the long-dead occupants of an aviary: birds of many feathers were perched upon its mountainous peak. Dickens may have wondered if the woman were not in some way a mobile graveyard for birds that had once played in the organic detritus of the street. Whatever she or her hat was, Dickens prepared himself, for no apparent reason, to join the woman outside the Fleggjoy's residence.

If Dickens had been capable of a deeper level of observation, he may well have remembered that this particular woman had often walked past the house, though until now she had always deemed it unnecessary to stop. He may also have remembered that, while passing, she had never missed an opportunity to hold her nose well and truly cloudward, and make a contemptuous 'Huff' under her breath. But, alas, Dickens was not given to such mental nuances, and he therefore did not notice that there was something quite different about the said woman this day, something that contradicted her former behaviour.

Having stopped at the front door, the woman with the hat of many dead birds said an internal prayer and then laid her delicate hand on the large and noble Fleggjoy knocker.

Just at that moment, Mrs Catalyst, the housekeeper, was making her weekly inspection of the downstairs broom cupboard and was therefore none too pleased at the interruption. With an impatient shake of the head and the hand, she allowed Mary momentarily to escape her inquisition to answer the call. 'And hurry up, girl,' she commanded the child as she continued her fault-finding routine.

Fully aware of the success of her actions, the plump woman's lower lip started to quiver as she heard the inner corridor resound to the echo of approaching footsteps. Being well acquainted with the corridor of old (before the days of the upstart Fleggjoys), she knew that there were but a few seconds left to adopt a mask of confident appearance. 'Oh, oh, oh,' she said to herself, at the same time rearranging the large birds' nest perched on her head. Pulling at her jacket and redistributing her pearls on her sagging bosom, she tried to calm her shivering spirit.

Had the woman bothered to look down at the hem of her voluminous skirt, she would have seen the eager and expectant figure of Dickens and might possibly have reflected on the irony of the family pet seeking the same entrance as a prominent neighbour. *Is it not strange*, she might have mused,

that in spite of all the social advances of recent times, one cannot teach a cat, a mere family appendage that knows nothing of honest labour or investments, to choose a different entrance than one enjoyed by the respectable?

But, if Dickens was no observer of the vagaries of the human condition, neither was the woman who now stood above him a reflector on the state of catdom. Even if she had noticed the small black and white fellow waiting so anxiously to gain entrance, she would have not given him more than a cursory glance – for her mind was full of matters of the gravest and greatest of gravity.

Mary opened the door and, without a thought, did a slight rear-lowering curtsey. This little sign of social inferiority immediately calmed somewhat the fluttering heart in the breast below the line of pearls and enabled the woman to speak more confidently than previously she might have managed.

'Is your master, Mr Fleggjoy, at home,' said the now only slightly shaking voice of the prominent neighbour, 'to – to – to receive Mrs Caselot Monkhaven Utterpout?' Mary gave another slight curtsey, and ushered Mrs Utterpout into the small anteroom where she very softly asked the lady to make ' 'erself comfy-table'.

On being left alone, while Mary went off to check the availability of Mr Fleggjoy, Mrs Utterpout did not 'make 'erself comfy-table'. Nor did she venture to 'make 'erself at home'. And though she had the pick of two sofas and three armchairs, she did not feel comfortable in any posture other than an upright one. No, in that house on that day there was nowhere that the troubled woman could rest herself, and the perpendicular was always the most reliable of postures at such times.

If the house were now strange to Mrs Utterpout, it was because she had chosen to be a stranger in it. When Mr and Mrs Utterpout, Mr and Mrs Ventnor Tiffgit, the Widow Featherthoughtly and all the other better people who lived in the neat stucco'd community of Periodic Square had found out that a mere promoted clerk had chosen to reside among them, a social *cordon sanitaire* had been slung up around the Fleggjoy abode as quickly as you could say 'social pariah'. It was Mrs Utterpout herself who had organised the embargo and proudly led the shunning of these lesser people. Thus the innumerable entreaties to come to this or that 'At Home' by Mr and Mrs Falstaff Fleggjoy had been studiously left unanswered, adding more than the usual insult to injury.

(Of course, when No. 17 had been owned by General Pierbrush Nukeley it had been a different affair. But the Pier-brush Nukeleys had 'gawn off' to Cheltenham to live among other military types who could talk all day and night about matters pertaining to soldiery and barricades. And in their wake, like some tide of unwanted and uncalled-for social change, had come the Fleggjoys.)

Mr Fleggjoy now bounded into the small anteroom with the energy of a man who was about to lay eyes on his oldest and most long-lost friend. 'Mrs Utterpout,' he screeched, prof-fering a firm hand to meet the gloved one of his distinguished visitor. 'Mrs Caselot Monkhaven Utterpout, 'ow charmin', 'ow devastatingly charmin'.'

Mr Fleggjoy's joy was, in its superabundance, quite contagious, and while he vigorously shook her hand, Mrs Utterpout gave the nearest thing to a spontaneous and equal demonstration of joy: 'Oh, sir, sir, what a pleasure. What a great and deep pleasure it is to see and meet you at last. What a great and deep pleasure it is.'

'Ah, madam,' said the host, 'why, I 'ad almost abandoned 'ope of ever seeing you in my own domicile,' as he indelicately squeezed Mrs Utterpout's hand. The squeeze, though not inflicting any physical damage to the limp and useless appendage, none the less alerted its owner to a sense of regret.

'Sir, I do hope I find you at home at this hour?' she added in a voice that deftly hid the underside of unease.

'Why, madam,' Mr Fleggjoy exploded into rhetorical posture, 'I am at 'ome whatever time your charmin' self requires me presence thereof.'

As Mr Fleggjoy attempted his verbal gyrations, Mrs Utterpout shuddered inwardly at the thought that this man was offering her 'open house'. Why, the man's manner, even on this first meeting, and in spite of having the finest house in Periodic Square, left a lot to be desired.

'Thank you, sir,' she mouthed. 'It is most charming of you, too ...' Here she faltered. For a moment she had not a pleasantry available to offer to the obsequious man before her. The very man whom she had previously so studiously avoided stood in front of her now like someone caught in a sudden downpour waiting for the aid of an umbrella. He hung there in his half-bent supplication with the smile of a pleased and expectant undertaker hoping for some jewel of bereavement. But Mrs Utterpout quickly regained her composure, drawing upon the countless years of social inanities piled up in her train. 'Ah, sir,' she began again, 'ah, sir, you are generosity incarnate, generosity itself.'

It having been established that Mr Fleggjoy was indeed 'at home', the prominent neighbour was welcomed into the family withdrawing room, and a feast of tea and elegant comestibles was ordered. While they waited for the arrival of the decorative edibles, they continued to swap pleasantries. As expected, the finest were uttered by Mrs Utterpout, who in her time had shaken hands with Lord Byron and had known the Prince Regent for a few minutes at Brighton.

'Mr Fleggjoy, you have indeed improved the old General's house. What a veritable treasure trove of furnishings and decorations! Why, I do believe that the General did not have a brush put to the woodwork for some twenty years, but you, sir, have made the place sparkle like a ... er, I do not know what!'

Mr Fleggjoy glowed in the warmth of the interminable compliments that his guest dusted down and utilized from her vast array of social niceties. Once in full swing they popped out like the 'flags of all nations', all tagged neatly and tidily, one after the other. Her deftness eventually so impressed both herself and the object of her compliments that the eyes of both of them glossed over in mutual wonder. (*From what deep cavern*, thought Mrs Utterpout, *do I manage to conjure up such travesties?*)

6

After what seemed to the purveyor of the travesties like an Atlantic of social dishonesties, the tea and delicacies finally arrived. *Fortunately*, Mrs Utterpout comforted herself, *I am on my own and am making these comments to someone who does not in the least matter*. It was, after all, an exercise to soften up the fellow and therefore her transgression of truth and true feeling was entirely necessary.

'Oh, sir, if you only knew how busy has been my time these last few years. So busy that, having had three brothers, a sister and numerous family pets die on me, I did not have the slightest opportunity of attending any of their interments. I venture to add that if my dear *mater* and *pater* themselves had passed on during these last few years (if, that is, they were not already happily ensconced in heaven), why, I would have had no chance at all to see them dispatched to eternity.'

Here she paused, conscious of the possibility that her tongue may have run so fast that even this upstart of a clerk might have noticed that she was inventing excuses at the speed of a mail coach on a downward parliamentary road.

'And the trouble I have had with staff! Why it is horrendous, *horr-ren-dous!* And would you believe it, sir, if I told you (in the strictest of confidence, of course) that not only were there two, if not three, illegitimate conceptions amongst my staff, but that on occasions they have thrown my social invitations into the kitchen fire! Whether more from bravado than spite I cannot say.'

Dickens, meanwhile, had taken himself through the cavernous interiors of the house down into the kitchen where, though perennially busy, Cook Bleery was to be relied upon. Sure enough, once he had cleared corridor, passage, stair and door Dickens found himself in the inviting kitchen standing before a bowl of possibly the finest victuals being offered to a member of the four-legged fraternity on that day in that year in that city. For, if the lot of the house reflected recent improvements in fortune, these also reflected in the small bowl that was put out for the family pet.

This day, the day when the important neighbour came to beg favours and forgiveness, Dickens was offered the finest of liver, though to be sure, there was little edge to his appetite. Thus when he had not even half-finished his meal, he turned away and sought exit from the kitchen, causing Cook Bleery to remonstrate with her charge.

'Ain't ye hungry, me fine fella?' she said with the soft lilt of a native from another isle. 'Or have ye been at the scurrilious long tails again?' To which Dickens could only look up at the large face of his provider as if in mock disconcern. The look may well have been interpreted by the ageing colleen as 'If it's so blidding great, why don't you blidding well eat it yourself.'

'Sure yer a divil of a fella, young Dickens, you are, with the world in such a state o' mortification for lack of nourishment.'

Dickens continued for a moment to accept Cook Bleery's banter, but he soon fell to scratching a vital part of his lower back. Then, standing, and with the swaggering walk of one who knows his place, he turned and left the steamy constraints of the kitchen to seek a cooler place to sleep away the afternoon. Mounting stairs and turning hither and thither, he was quickly back in the hall. Outside the family drawing room, in which great sociabilities were being perpetrated, Dickens sat and licked a piece of paw and a bit of leg until the chance of gaining entry to the room inevitably presented itself.

Dickens' vigil was of short duration as, very soon, a maid appeared to bring refreshment to the teapot. When the door was opened, Dickens quickly entered and surveyed the room. Sitting in a large armchair by the bow window was the plump woman and opposite, on a small though comfortable sofa, sat the master of the house.

Dickens made a balletic leap on to one of the fleet of chairs, and in so doing chanced to catch the eye of the plump woman with the hat of many deaths.

'Oh, oh,' she screeched with the power of a mariner falling from a crow's nest, and pointed towards Dickens, now safely settled on the chair. 'If I have ever seen a finer cat,' she began her panegyric, 'then my eyes have been well deceived.'

Her instant enthusiasm for the family pet filled the heart of Mr Fleggjoy with pride, as he reasoned that you could judge the truthfulness of people by how they responded to children and animals. And as he was childless, for someone to declare love for Mr Fleggjoy's pride and joy – Dickens – was a royal road to his already happy heart.

Unfortunately Dickens had no time for the declarations of perfection issuing from the woman, as he quickly prepared himself for a light sleep that would soon turn into something of a deeper nature.

In the meanwhile, Mrs Utterpout, having softened up her host, alighted on the subject that was the ulterior purpose of her visit – and lo and behold, if it were not the life and death question of finance.

During the previous three years, the Utterpouts had watched with astonishment as the Fleggjoy household sprouted not only the obvious signs of success, but also the obvious signs of plenty. 'But where does all the money come from?' Mr Utterpout had often asked his wife. 'The man has no background, eh? No class, eh? No nothing, eh? But money aplenty, eh?' Mr Utterpout's moustache bristled all the more as he witnessed the gradual transformation of the decaying No. 17 into the most splendid of houses. And then one day the old gentleman suggested that his spouse call on Mr Fleggjoy and seek his advice about investments: while the tired old dividends they received each year seemed to be diminishing, a few doors from them there was a man of mean beginnings who was apparently flourishing.

'You must call on him, madam,' Mr Utterpout had said that very morning. And now here she was, swallowing her pride, truth and dignity in the interests of borrowing some of the financial sunshine of the once-miserable clerk and rejected neighbour.

'Please bear in mind, madam,' said the former clerk, now on his favourite subject, 'that investments can go down as well as up.'

Dickens stirred in his sleep, brushed an imaginary long

tail away from his face and pounced into a jungle made up entirely of the pointed tails of small animals.

And Mrs Utterpout finished her twelfth sandwich.

2

A Certain
and
Irrational Fear

Once Mrs Utterpout had finished her last sandwich and uttered her final inanity, she left the house in a state of rosy, overfed pleasure. As the front door closed behind her, Mr Fleggjoy's nervous but excited partner came mouse-like down from an upstairs room.

'Mr Fleggjoy,' she asked excitedly, in an undecided state of hope and fear, 'what brought her unannounced to our 'umble door?' ' 'umble' it was not, but the nervous woman let the word slip out before realizing its inappropriateness. Mr Fleggjoy then set about giving her the fullest of accounts, not forgetting to mention that she had much admired their cat Dickens.

'She was very much taken by 'im, my dear,' he said with obvious pleasure. 'Much taken indeed.'

'I am sure she was much taken, sir,' Mrs Fleggjoy replied rather curtly, 'but what else was she taken by? Was she taken by the curtains, and the carpet, which cost us an arm and a leg in the getting? And what 'ad she to say about the new sideboard which cost us a king's ransom?'

Mr Fleggjoy did his best to describe the nature of the visit, adding that it had not been made in order to take an inventory of their worldly goods. But to all intents and purposes, Mrs Fleggjoy was convinced of nothing more than that her husband had omitted much detail in his description.

She persisted: 'And what did she say about the armchairs, and the new sofa which I chose the coverin's meself

11

for, out of a choice of no less than forty very expensive materials?'

But Mr Fleggjoy could say no more than that the tea had gone 'appreciably well' and that Mrs Utterpout had been forcibly struck by the improvements made by them to the house since the days of the former owners.

'Of course she was impressed,' said his wife in exasperation. 'Why, it was no more than a blidding shell when the old gent and his missus moved out. I tell you, Mr Fleggjoy, she must 'ave kept her eyes closed if she did not at least mention the carpet and the curtains.'

'Well, all I can say, madam,' said her husband, now near to irritation at the cross-questioning, 'that she was mighty impressed, mighty impressed indeed.' To which his wife could only say rather sourly, 'And what evidence d'you 'ave for that sir, when she said 'ardly a word about anything? Not even about the curtains and carpets.'

Mr Fleggjoy, refusing to be pressed further, settled for a stern increase of emphasis in his voice as he insisted that nothing had escaped their guest's eye, but that as she was as polite as 'a lady-in-waiting to the Royal 'ousehold', Mrs Utterpout would, of course, forgo all comment. Unfortunately, all this elicited from his agitated partner was a rolling of eyes towards heaven and the comment that men were not the best judges of a woman's reasoning.

It was a good hour before the discussion drew to an inconclusive halt, by which time Dickens had risen from his slumber and desired an exit. As usual, he had slept through the weaving of another few strands of life's rich tapestry. Once out of the drawing room where the echo of insistence could still be read in Mrs Fleggjoy's voice, he made for the kitchen and the business of dispatching the remnants of the liver. Back below stairs, Cook Bleery again managed a wry comment from her storehouse of them, this time along the lines that the conquering hero was returned. She then took some milk from the pitcher and filled his little milk bowl, and then added a few morsels to the now slightly curling liver. 'You are a lord on this earth,' Cook Bleery said as she stood above her charge, who as usual was tucking in with an economy of ceremony. In no time at all, Dickens had sated his appetite and sought exit through the kitchen door into the garden.

Once there, Dickens disappeared into the undergrowth. Among bush, tree and long grass he immediately disturbed the security of a number of small furry animals as he practised his primaeval need to hunt. He was no doubt intent on dispatching a long tail to a premature end, but such was the gloom of the dusk-time that little record of the event could be made by the human eye. Thus into the dark went Dickens, the murderer of small and frightened things, as the lights went on around Periodic Square.

Back in the house, as if to escape from the idea that he had ineffectually run the meeting with the social titan, Mr Fleggjoy returned again by the light of the gas lamp to all he could manage to remember. But this was still not enough for the troubled mistress of the house and she pleaded for something more tangible than that which her husband had offered. It was, in fact, this further pleading that jogged her partner's memory. 'Why yes, madam,' he said excitedly, 'there was another something that entirely slipped my mind. Mrs Utterpout said that, subject to a check in her diary at 'ome she would most 'opefully be inviting us to tea tomorrow afternoon.'

Instead of quietening his spouse's agitated breast, this last piece of information, dredged up from the very bottom of Mr Fleggjoy's memory, drove her into near turmoil, leading her to protest most loudly that not only had she not a thing to wear, but she was not ready for *real* gentry. ' 'ow can I meet with my social betters, sir, without advance preparation?'

'Do not be foolish, madam,' replied Mr Fleggjoy sternly. 'You are as good a woman as any in this exalted square,' to which his wife could not agree. Further assurances of the supremacy not only of her wardrobe but of her gentility had little effect in calming her troubled mind.

'Tea? Tomorrow?' she bawled. 'It's too soon, too too soon.' At this moment of high-pitched hysteria, Mary brought in an envelope on a little silver salver.

'Mrs Utterpout's servant, madam, 'as just left this.'

The coincidence of the crescendo of hysteria and the arrival of the invitation was less than fortuitous for Mrs Fleggjoy, who had changed from her usual happy pink to a deep and troubled crimson. Mr Fleggjoy took the ivory-coloured envelope and dismissed Mary. Carefully opening it, he removed the finely printed card it contained and read the elegant copperplate of Mrs Caselot Monkhaven Utterpout. They had awaited such an invitation for what had seemed like a lifetime, but now that it had arrived, their consternation could be cut with a knife.

Mrs Fleggjoy spent a restless night, tormented by the fact that, on the morrow, she would have to meet with the woman she feared more than any other. The social titan would read her like a book and in the reading would see that if Mrs Fleggjoy did not lack wealth and its trinkets, she did lack breeding and polish. 'Oh, for the life of me, what *am* I going to do?'

Some time in the early hours, while her husband slept contentedly, she got out of bed and, going to the window, looked out on the vast dark stillness of Periodic Square. Was this, all this, what she wanted? Was all this what she had looked forward to and struggled for in the days of their stricter regime? In those grim but honest days at Dumpling Passage?

After some minutes of painful soul-searching Mrs Fleggjoy returned to her snoring husband, resolving to do all she could to make the next day's social event as trouble-free as possible. But deep within her she realized that her rise from respectable aspirant to plenty was about to be sorely tested.

As she pulled the clean linen sheets over her she could hear in the square below the squabbling of cats, one of whom she imagined to be the small fellow who graced their house. *It's all well and good,* she thought to herself, *for her to be impressed by a cat. A cat can come from a good 'ome or a bad 'ome, a rich 'ome or a poor 'un. But who can tell the difference with most cats? Does a cat take to wearing better clothes to show its rank? Does it start talking about culture and things?*

Of course it don't. For a cat is a cat is a cat.

With this profundity on the classlessness of cats, she turned over in bed and set her mind to sleeping, though sleep itself did not overcome her until the first bird had heralded the dawn and the milkman's cart was below in the early spring morning square. Then she finally slipped into a state near to slumber with her mind full of the deepest and ugliest feelings of social inadequacy she had ever suffered.

The squabbling cats ceased their altercation. Soon after, Dickens gained entry through the kitchen door, courtesy of Cook Bleery who once again commented on the sweet and charmed life of a cat. 'And what has our little villain been up to this past night?' she enquired of Dickens as he awaited the ladling of some milk into his bowl.

Save for the noise of the lapping cat and the busy cook in the kitchen and the rising of young maids in the loftier regions of the house, all was quiet and still. Mrs Fleggjoy, though, turned over in her troubled mind the picture of herself standing at a crossroads in the city, completely bereft of clothing.

3

A Touch
of
Class

Late the next afternoon, Dickens strolled into the square, now absent of warring birds. The last of the equestrian ordure was in the process of being cleared up, and any enticement to sparrow and starling would go with the cart. Dickens walked along the pavement hoping to see something of interest. His day had been spent in places other than the square and thus his return would soon require him to seek entrance to the family house. Sitting outside the large front door, he awaited his opportunity, though he would have stood a better chance of entry from the garden. But it was Dickens' nature to do what he wanted to do rather than do what was supposedly obvious.

On the opposite side of the square, he suddenly noticed two familiar figures coming out of a house not dissimilar to the Fleggjoy abode. Dickens sat and concentrated. *Is this*, he seemed to think, *my own master and mistress, Mr and Mrs Falstaff Fleggjoy?*

Sure enough, once they had bid goodbye to their host and hostess on the steps of the house, they turned and walked towards No. 17. Dickens could clearly recognize the rolling gait of his mistress and the short, almost pigeon-toed steps of his master, the one a short, bulging woman, the other a man who, although tall and slight, had a portly bulge to his middle.

Dickens observed them intently as they walked, for this was indeed a new phenomenon. Rarely, if ever, had he seen his

master and mistress out in the square, especially leaving a neighbouring house. Even when Mr Fleggjoy went to the office, he did so by carriage, and on the rare occasions that Mrs Fleggjoy ventured out, it was also in the same vehicle. To all intents and purposes, they were 'carriage folk' and never went out in the day or a night unless in that conveyance.

It did not take even this slow-walking couple long to reach the front door of No. 17. Mrs Fleggjoy was the first to notice the family cat and, bending, stroked him as though he were some token of their good luck, if not an emissary of further benevolent fortune.

''allo, my little spoilt pet. 'ow have you been spending your day?' The strokes were genuine but exaggerated by the obvious joy felt by the mistress of the house in being finally free of the Utterpouts' residence.

Mr Fleggjoy took out his key and let the three of them into the house. As soon as the door was opened, what had been a residence of calm waiting turned instantly into a hive of great activity. A maid and the butler ran about, as well as the housekeeper, aware that the master and mistress had returned home.

Mrs Fleggjoy was helped off with her light summer jacket and Mr Fleggjoy gave up his walking stick and hat. 'Thank you, Tetley,' said the master to the butler and then followed Mrs Fleggjoy up the stairs.

Dickens did not wait on ceremony but proceeded to the kitchen for his assignation with the provider of his first meal of the day. It was Cook's day off so it fell on Mrs Catalyst to set out the food, a task that she rather liked performing for the family pet.

'Oh, my sweet,' she said as she filled his bowl of milk and gave him the nourishment Cook Bleery had prepared for that day. It was beef and was tolerably well accepted by Dickens, who consumed it with the speed of lightning as Mrs Catalyst stood above him and admired all there was to admire about a healthy cat in the middle of healthy consumption.

Mrs Fleggjoy, meanwhile, had changed into something

less formal and sat at her dressing table while her husband did likewise in his dressing room. Once united in the marital bedroom, they gave each other the kind of smiles that for the uninitiated might have been described as crazed.

'Oh, sir,' began the mistress, 'I believe that Mrs Utterpout is an 'ighly commendable person who ought to be blessed for her genny-ross-city.'

'A cap'tal woman,' replied her spouse, 'and her 'usband, Mr Utterpout, is not far behind in goodness.' They grinned maniacally before Mr Fleggjoy went over to his wife and, in the manner of a French aristocrat kissing the neck of his mistress, began pecking at his partner's thick red neck. She giggled and coughed, and then unexpectedly broke out into a deep gurgling sob which took her husband totally by surprise.

'Mrs Fleggjoy! Mrs Fleggjoy! What means this? Are you un'appy, madam?' at which his wife turned and whacked him so hard on the shoulder that he nearly went down.

'Sad, sir? Sad? Why this 'as been the happiest day of my whole blidding life. My whole blidding life.' And then she fell into her husband's arms, causing him almost to collapse, having only partially recovered from the bruising clump he had just received.

'Sir, I do not know that there is nothing that could ever make me 'appier.' And then the deep sobs of happiness really began in earnest, and before Mr Fleggjoy was aware of it, his shoulder and upper jacket were soaked through with the tears of his most happy wife. There they stood, motionless, for a few minutes, though every now and then his wife would take her red-cheeked face out of the snug corner formed by Mr Fleggjoy's neck and shoulder and declare herself again to be at the pinnacle of life's bliss. 'I couldn't be 'appier!' she periodically reassured him between wails.

Downstairs, many of the loud noises from the marital bedroom found echo and alarmed the staff. Was the mistress ill? they asked each other. And if she were not ill, what was all the wailing and gnashing for? Mrs Catalyst, the sometime captain of the house, walked up to the bedroom door and, knocking tentatively, politely asked if there were anything she could do. To which Mr Fleggjoy could only thank her and say that there was nothing. But Mrs Fleggjoy's realization that her faithful retainer was in the hall looking for ways she could assist brought further wailing and gnashing culminating in Mrs Fleggjoy rushing to the door and embracing Mrs Catalyst as though she were her long-lost sister.

'Oh, Mrs Catalyst, Mrs Catalyst, thank you, thank you!' she shouted in her housekeeper's ear, 'but it be 'appiness that brings me out in tears.' And then she ventured to say that, what with her happiness and staff like Mrs Catalyst, her cup did genuinely runneth over.

Mrs Catalyst returned below stairs with a look of great surprise and a rather damp area in the snug corner formed by her neck and shoulder. In this state of heightened awareness, she told the other staff that it was happiness that had brought the mistress out to yelping and screeching and not, as they had imagined, some deep, unfathomable despair.

Dickens sat dutifully awaiting an exit at the first possible moment from the hall into the drawing room. Mrs Catalyst finally saw the little fellow and, having apologized at least three times, allowed him in. Once in the room, Dickens made for his favourite chair and proceeded to take a well-deserved nap. And there he stayed until the tear-washed Mrs Fleggjoy and the mildly elated Mr Fleggjoy came in to sit and read the newspaper and discuss further the events of the afternoon.

It was jointly agreed that the afternoon had been a great success and that Mrs Utterpout was an instant and sincere best friend. As for Mr Utterpout, why he was the personification of all that was good about the English upper classes, polite almost to a fault.

The evening went on as it had begun. Mr Fleggjoy would try to concentrate on the newspaper or one of his novels (which he read for self-improvement), but could not fail to return to the subject of the audience that they had had that very afternoon. Mrs Fleggjoy likewise was sidetracked from her normal needlework. 'Oh, Mr Fleggjoy, I think she is a duchess if there ever was one.' Mr Fleggjoy could only nod in agreement.

Fortunately, none of the emotional histrionics of the afternoon was played out again in the peace of the night. Tranquillity had returned to the household, though Mrs Fleggjoy did send a hurried message off to her sister at Bishopsgate to attend her the following morning on a matter of the most importance. As the sister was beholden to Mrs Fleggjoy in more ways than one, she was sure to attend. So as the night drew to a close, Mrs Fleggjoy had the delicious task of planning what to tell her sister on the morrow of the splendid Utterpouts, who had in their time not only known Lord Byron well but had been intimate with the Prince Regent for a number of seasons at Brighton.

Dickens awoke from his deep slumbers, yawned, scratched and then, on bringing to Mr Fleggjoy's notice the desire to depart, awaited him at the drawing room door. Mr Fleggjoy, ever willing to oblige, opened the door and let out Dickens into the hall and then opened the front door so that his little pet could saunter out into the sharp night air. Once in Periodic Square, the cat surveyed the scene and then set his mind on a walk beyond the square's confines to other, less salubrious districts.

And thus another day ended for the Fleggjoy partnership. That it had been an auspicious day could not be denied. That it had been a strange day full of the unexpected would possibly have been the opinion of the staff, if canvassed. But to Dickens it had been but another day in the life of a cat in his prime. Events may come and events may go, but the diurnal and nocturnal rounds of the cat were as predictable as the rising of the moon.

And, to be sure, there was this night a full moon.

4
In the Beginning
was
Dumpling Passage

(The story of Dickens, the hero of these pages, is as intertwined with the house of Fleggjoy as is the ivy that binds itself to the mighty oak.)

Dumpling Passage was one of those lost places that huddle beyond the light of day a stone's throw from Fleet Street and the perambulations of respectable folk. If one were to disappear up an alley from the main thoroughfare and make some tortuous manoeuvres through the narrow ways, one might, with a stroke or two of luck, happen upon this closeted little place. But many who had set out intent upon arriving never succeeded. If one were to ask a passing fellow, 'Excuse me, I am looking for Dumpling Passage,' the answer might itself be a question: 'And what would you want at Dumpling Passage?'

What one wanted in that particular passage – or any one of the many that ran like badly designed ribs from the backbone of Fleet Street – would be a hard question to answer, as the respectable seldom ventured to such parts. If the respectable did desire something from one of those who lived within the labyrinth, one sent one's bailiffs with the aid of a peeler or two and a few large sticks as the necessary accoutrements to such a jaunt into the hinterland. And even then, one was not entirely assured of success.

But that is not to say that only the most hardened recidivists lived within the warren of which Dumpling Passage was a part. If the passage was the home of the fallen, it was also the home of a great many of the yet-to-have-risen. 'You wait, my love' might be the sentiments of one: 'As soon as Aunt Dorothea is no more than a memory, there will be prosperity aplenty.'

Thus this passage held the hopes and aspirations of many, as well as the criminal imaginations of the few. In one particular aspirant household, a certain cat called Augusta, blessed with the best of catly looks, lived as the family pet. But as will happen, nature will have its way, and Augusta was often 'productive'. That her productivity was always looked upon as a fall, a slip, rather than as part of some grand plan, meant that the master and mistress were continually seeking homes for her progeny. That is, until her last attempt at mother-hood, when all her offspring bar one were quickly dispatched to homes in the neighbourhood. The remaining little chap was scheduled to join the household of a particular nightwatchman, who was desirous of another cat. But, alas, misfortune struck when, one night, the nightwatchman caught a heavy chill, and it was not long after that he went to a place where cats and braziers were of little import. As luck would have it, the lost kitten was therefore permitted to stay in the house in which he had been born, and thus he became the younger Fleggjoy cat, a role that he soon set out to fulfil with great dignity and cunning. Dickens, as the fellow was soon named, was awarded an honour, for when the time came for his dear mother to 'pass on' he, Dickens, would take her place as the senior Fleggjoy cat.

Within the sound of the bells of St Bride's, Dumpling Passage held within its narrow confines as variegated a range of humanity as one would find in any city. At one end of the passage lived a class of person to whom strong drink was a much used though temporary elixir. On any day of the year, a Mrs Hemlock, for instance, might take a stick to a Mr Hemlock's head with the intention of beating some sobriety and sense into it. Such pedagogic exercises might in themselves prove useless, but this did not stop the said Mrs Hemlock from laying her large, heavy stick about the head of her spouse as soon as

24

he was so drunk that sensible words and coordinated movement failed him. Likewise, a Mr Approbation might take it into his head to try and dance the polka with a broomstick in the hope of demonstrating to all assembled that, in his day, he had been a fair carouser at society dances.

But one had only to walk a few yards and there clustered were the simple aspirants who desired no more than respectability and a future. In these few households congregated at one end of the passage, one met the threadbare hardworking, the very backbone and the best of England. Among this number grew the honest root, surprisingly untouched or untarnished by its close proximity to evil and greed.

In this upright, small corner of Dumpling Passage, the most upright and abstemious in all matters was the Fleggjoy household. Although the couple had been destined by Providence to be childless, they none the less aspired to better things.

Yes, central to the Fleggjoy beginnings was Dumpling Passage to which, some years before, the young Falstaff Fleggjoy had brought his young bride, determined that sobriety, hard work and early rising would give them all that inheritance had not. 'One day, my dear,' he would often say, 'we shall, through 'ard work and application, better ourselves. Yes, you will see we shall, if my name is not Falstaff Fleggjoy.' To which his 'treasure' would always indicate her approval: 'I shall look forward to that, sir.'

And Falstaff Fleggjoy was a man of his very word. In the twenty years that he laboured at his desk in the service of the younger Delloyt of Slaughterfoot, Cockensie & Delloyt, his position improved from that of meagre clerk to that of senior clerk. Mr Fleggjoy's endless struggle to make sense of ledgers and monies was rewarded by a growing realization in the minds of the extant partners that their clerk was as committed to the prosperity of the business as they were. At the end of each passing year, Mr Fleggjoy was dutifully called into the younger Delloyt's office to receive a further recognition of his growing importance, an importance that Mr Fleggjoy valued as much as he valued the steady, though modest, increments that he received in remuneration for his loyalty and effort.

Mrs Fleggjoy likewise prospered in the shadow, though not in the shade, of her dedicated husband, for she was as wedded to his ideals and ambitions as she was to the man himself. Not a bristle hair could come between them and their desire to lift themselves one day from the respectable but not entirely inspiring circumstances of Dumpling Passage.

A less patient couple might have given up after twenty years, but not the Fleggjoys. They stoically carried on their four-handed struggle, like two mountaineers roped together in a slow, almost invisible creep up to the summit. They would get there one day, they told themselves, and all their effort would lead eventually to reward.

Such was the Fleggjoy lot until – as if mysteriously connected with their acceptance that Dickens was to join the family on a permanent footing – their world was turned arsy-versy. All their plans, all the long abstemious years were rudely tossed aside with the indifference of a wave destroying a child's paper boat.

Dickens, this day when the world changed, was in the small Fleggjoy kitchen learning the art of washing himself in between enjoying the benefits of his mother's milk. This had been his regime for all the days of his short life, but this day his toilet was performed against the backdrop of great events.

It was late afternoon when Mr Fleggjoy came in, breath-less and before time, from his employers' office at Lincoln's Inn. His spouse sat in the parlour mending a tablecloth that, though it had seen long service both in her own household and that of her mother, could with attention still have a few more years' life left in it. The sight of her husband rushing through the parlour door came as a shock. Being a woman of great labour and routine, she knew the time of day without so much as looking at the mantelpiece clock.

'Madam,' began the man breathlessly, 'madam, I am 'ome.'

'I can see you are at 'ome, sir,' she replied. 'And I can

see that you have done so ahead of the clock.' She put down the tablecloth and rose from her chair as if to be in a more equitable position to take in the unprecedented appearance of her husband ahead of the normal time. But as she stood up, her husband collapsed into a chair and, in collapsing, dropped forward onto the table as though he had lost control of his upper parts.

'Mr Fleggjoy,' she demanded, 'what is this?' For a moment the image of her husband standing before a large tankard of porter formed in her mind as the only possible explanation for this collapse. But she pushed that image forcibly aside and came quickly to the conclusion that her husband was unwell.

'Sir, you are unwell?'

' "Unwell", madam?' replied her husband, now endeavouring to pull himself upright in the chair. But then his voice deserted him and, looking hard into his wife's face, he began to cry. And not just to cry but to add to it a kind of whimpering sound, the like of which you might hear from a dog that, after excessive punishment, has run out of yelps.

Amazement, fear and astonishment all caught Mrs Fleggjoy by the throat. She stood above her husband who had been reduced to a jelly of quivering inelegance. *What can I do?* she thought. *'as this ever 'appened before?* It had not, and the only thing she could think of was to do what her mother had done on a few occasions to her drunken husband. So, bending down, Mrs Lulucia Fleggjoy grasped her puny husband by the elbows and, pulling him towards her, scowled into his face and shouted at him to pull himself together. 'Sir! Sir!' she bellowed. 'What kind of behaviour is this for a man full grown and in his prime? Eh?' To which her husband could make no coherent reply from the depths of his crying.

The dreadful sounds of bellowing and whimpering in the parlour travelled clearly into the kitchen. Augusta, one could imagine, suspecting that a murder was in progress in the next room, stood sentinel beside her young offspring. Dickens was entirely unconcerned with the commotion, busy playing with

a ball of paper while his mother's eyes grew wide and worried. Looking towards the door, did she half expect that, at any moment, a lunging lunatic would appear clutching a large breadknife dripping with the blood of her mistress?

The day that the Fleggjoy chariot changed direction, Augusta was more concerned about protecting her offspring than she was of the mental condition of the persons in the other room. But in that other room, the mistress standing above the master was more than a little alarmed by the lack of response her husband made to her shaking and hollering. Mrs Fleggjoy, having made no impact with her vigorous physical and verbal assault, now decided to go to the opposite extreme and put her large meaty arms around her distressed spouse. 'Sir, Mr Fleggjoy, what ails you, my dear?'

' "Ails" me?' echoed Mr Fleggjoy, now looking up deeply into the eyes of Mrs Fleggjoy. 'Why, nothing,' he managed before he collapsed again into the whimpering and crying posture of before.

Such manifestations encouraged Augusta to grab her offspring, much to his surprise, by the loose skin on his neck and take him into the cupboard where, some weeks before, he had been born. There, within the darkness, Augusta looked anxiously at her puzzled fledgling and listened to the noises outside. And there they sat as the drama unfolded beyond.

Having made no progress with either the stern or the conciliatory approach, Mrs Fleggjoy walked around her sagging, sobbing husband and folded and unfolded her arms in consternation. *What in 'eaven's name is this?* she wondered. ' *'as this man gone to the dogs?'*

The whimpering abated. Mrs Fleggjoy sat beside her husband and held his hand whilst she murmured the kinds of sounds one would to a child who had had a nightmare. Slowly Mr Fleggjoy returned to some control of his emotions and, looking up at his wife, managed to put a few words together.

'Madam, madam ... we 'ave been ... been smiled ... upon.'

' "Smiled upon"?' she enquired with a look of puzzlement.

'Who's smiled upon us, sir?'

'Providence, madam, Providence.'

Providence? she inwardly questioned. *Is this an insurance company that has blessed us with the early maturation of a forgotten policy? Or has some distant relative shuffled off their mortal coil and left us with a little bit of a legacy, maybe enough to recurtain the parlour?* 'Providence' was of little use to Mrs Fleggjoy, so she cast it aside and sought from her husband something more than this word. 'What do you mean, sir?' she asked.

Augusta was about to leave the bolt hole and take Dickens back to his unending game with the paper ball, but almost asshe resolved to do so and was sticking her nose through the cupboard door, a great shriek that dwarfed all previous sounds cut the air in half. If the previous noises had been worrying, this new one was terrifying. The element of danger that accompanies all loud reports caused even Dickens to shudder and huddle in the darkest, most protected part of the hideout. And there the two cats cowered while, beyond, mortifying sounds rang loud and true.

Augusta and Dickens stayed for another six months in Dumpling Passage after the day of loud reports, then Mr Fleggjoy found a fine house to purchase not far from their abode, but in an entirely different realm. In the new residence the Fleggjoys hoped to demonstrate that they were a partnership that could not only make the most of frugality but could also make the most of its polar opposite: immeasurable plenty.

Mr Fleggjoy had returned home that memorable day with the good news that his modest little investments had suddenly burgeoned into untold wealth. And with it the recognition that, as a man of substance, he could no longer remain as head clerk at the business of Slaughterfoot, Cockensie and Delloyt. Therefore from the morrow he was to be made a full partner. Slaughterfoot, Cockensie, Delloyt & Fleggjoy sounded much more convincing (it was intimated by the younger Delloyt) than the previous triumvirate.

5
Better Times

Despite appearances, luck is not always on the side of the well-made transmogrified cat. Even our hero Dickens sometimes had to wait in the limbo of the Fleggjoy hallway to gain access to his favourite resting place. In these better times, when plenty was plenteous, he would, as cats have since time immemorial, pass the odd hour licking, scratching and sitting.

On this particular day, Dickens sat outside the Fleggjoy drawing room and, with the patience of Job, waited to gain entrance while, within, the master and mistress discussed the day's plans.

'Tell me, madam,' asked Mr Fleggjoy on this bright day in the second year of the young Queen's ascendancy, ''ow long 'as it been since our increase?' As he waited for his wife's reply, Mr Fleggjoy stood half observing his image in the large mirror over the mantelpiece. With his hands behind his back and his chin stuck out, he was profoundly pleased with what he believed was his genteel appearance. An appearance, we might add, that never ceased to amaze and fascinate him.

Mrs Fleggjoy smiled and gave a middle-aged woman's version of a girlish giggle. 'Why, sir, 'owever long it's been, it's been a parry-dice.' She giggled again and stood beside him so that she, too, could also admire herself in the well-appointed mirror.

'Madam,' Mr Fleggjoy said after they had spent a moment's curtailment of talk to survey their respective images,

'I think you should be made cognizant of the fact that today is, if I might say so, a very special day.'

But, in fact, Mr Fleggjoy's original question had needed no answer. Rather, it was a way of alerting his loving wife that this ordinary day was about to turn into one of those special occasions. On such days, they would abandon the city and go out into its environs in their handsome carriage, there to indulge in the delights of a chop house or hotel menu.

Ahead of her husband, Mrs Fleggjoy began to think aloud, 'Shall we go off to Tott'num to see me Auntie Perilee, Mr Fleggjoy?' Aunt Perilee was a particular favourite as visiting her gave them the pleasure of being much admired by a less fortunate stratum of the family. 'Or shall we take ourselves to 'ampstead? To my cousin Nelly? Aye, that would be a joy, Mr Fleggjoy, eh?'

'As you wish, madam, it is your task to choose.'

Mrs Fleggjoy imagined a crude map of London. *Should we go north to Tott'num? Or nor'west to 'ampstead?* But then it suddenly occurred to her that there was one place she wished to go to more than anywhere else in the whole of the kingdom.

'Sir, if it is all right with you,' she said excitedly, 'I feel a trip to the Star 'n' Garter at Richmond 'ill could not be improved upon.' To which Mr Fleggjoy gave a slight bow to indicate that her wish was his command.

'Oh, sir, that would be capi-toll, capi-toll. As long as it is with your approval?' To which Mr Fleggjoy gave another little bow indicating that he concurred with all things to do with his splendid companion (which, if the truth were known, was far from true).

The bows and the giggles dispensed with, the Fleggjoys fell to some more moments of gazing at themselves in the grand mirror. Though Mr Fleggjoy had inherited his father's meaty hands, and his ears were decidedly large and hairy in the manner of a bucolic, his dress overcame much of the appearance of a successful pig farmer. With the aid of his tight waistcoat and fine frockcoat he looked like someone who lived off his investments and interest in a prominent firm of

London brokers.

Alas, Mrs Fleggjoy had more obvious signs than largeness of hand and ear to delineate her as an ex-member of the underclasses. In spite of the trappings of plenty, she always remained in appearance a working woman dressed up in her best 'day off' clothes, out to take a saunter through the streets. An unkind observation might be that not even a revolution would create the desired effect, so plebian was her general countenance.

Mr Fleggjoy, having exhausted interest in his own image for the moment, chanced to glance at the mirror image of his wife. What he saw left him feeling uneasy. Whereas his own sombre sartoria stamped him, if not a complete gentleman, then at least as an acceptable counterfeit, Mrs Fleggjoy betrayed certain disturbing signs. A counterfeit of a gentleman was perfectly acceptable in many areas of society, but not a small, plump, gaudy woman whose only dress sense was to spend 'an arm and a leg'. In short, Mrs Fleggjoy seemed not to have carved a new appearance for herself out of the opportunities presented by a ready supply of the wherewithal.

Having recently conquered the heights of social acceptance, Mr Fleggjoy intended now to take full advantage of these new connections. Having assisted Mr and Mrs Utterpout (and their investments were going along swimmingly), why not, he mused, ask the great lady for some assistance in redesigning his wife's tawdry appearance? This, of course, would have to be achieved diplomatically, but Mrs Utterpout was a truly wonderful woman who, Mr Fleggjoy was convinced, would with discretion and sympathy remodel his lumpish and ungainly wife.

Mr Fleggjoy did feel a certain pain in even thinking the unthinkable about the woman who had been the linchpin of their aspirancy. *Where would I be today*, he said to himself, *without that noble woman beside me?* He would thus do nothing that compromised their wondrous and fulsome relationship. A little bit of icing on the sartorial cake, though, would not go amiss, and this, more than anything, would bring his happiness to total and utter completion.

In the meanwhile, Mrs Fleggjoy had given up her contemplation of her image in the mirror and noticed that her husband was lost in thought.

'Is everything all right, sir?' she asked.

'Oh, yes, madam,' said Mr Fleggjoy, dismissing the uncomfortable reflections from his mind. Turning away from the mirror, he smiled at his wife with all the tenderness that he could muster. 'Of course, madam,' he replied, 'there is not a cloud on the 'orizon.'

'The Star 'n' Garter, sir, is one a me fav'rites.' She smiled like a child about to be given a choice between three coloured balloons.

Mr Fleggjoy now became determined to throw his heart and soul into the celebratory side of the day and to cast out dark and unresolved thoughts.

'Do you know, madam, the significance of this very special day?' he asked with a look of only slightly manufactured excitement.

'I know it's special, sir, but blow me if I knows the number.'

'Well, madam, it is none other than a three'er.'

'A three'er?' questioned Mrs Fleggjoy, 'why, it seems only a matter o' weeks ago it was a two'er.'

'Indeed, madam, a three'er. Three years, three months, three weeks and three days since fortune smiled on us. And Mr Delloyt, in recognition' – but he need say no more. They both understood the significance of that moment some three years since when their world had been remade. Now, returning to the memory of that special day, a little tear lodged itself in the corner of Mr Fleggjoy's eye. Looking down at his wife, he could not but be moved by the circumstances he now contemplated.

'Ah sir, you *are* a soft man,' said his spouse, noticing the evidence of emotion welling up from his soul. 'You are a softer man than ever there was.'

She took his beefy white hand and, squeezing it, brought

34

forth a few more trickles, causing her to take a kerchief from her sleeve and dab away the little evidences of her husband's softness.

Mr Fleggjoy now went to a little desk in the corner of the room and, opening a drawer with a key that hung from his watch chain, took out some large pieces of paper. Carefully he counted out one hundred pounds and, relocking his desk, folded the money and placed it in his pocket.

'We shall, madam,' he mumbled, still with a touch of emotion to his voice, 'call on the Institute on the way back and deposit with them some token of our belief in their good work.'

'Of course, sir, of course.'

Well-pleased smiles crossed both of their happy faces as they thought of all the good work that the 'Home for the Resettlement of Destitute Laundresses' would do with their modest contribution. And as the female members of Mrs Fleggjoy's family had been laundresses since the days of yore, it seemed only right to support those who had fallen on hard times.

Mr Fleggjoy now began to adjust his cravat. Mrs Fleggjoy pulled the bell to summon Mary, who soon arrived and was instructed to tell Jenks to get the carriage ready for a journey 'forthwith'. Having set the day's activities in train, Mrs Fleggjoy took her leave to make herself ready for the trip to the south-western suburbs of the city.

With the door at last opened, Dickens took the opportunity to enter. Once inside, he sat by the unlit hearth and looked up at his master, who was busy flicking imaginary specks of dust from his shoulders. It might have occurred to Dickens that his master was a little too preoccupied with his own reflection, but no trace of censor was visible on the cat's little black countenance.

Mr Fleggjoy finished his labours and, turning, spotted Dickens looking up at him. 'Oh,' the master began, 'so you 'ave deemed it time to return to us, 'ave you not?' to which Dickens could only register agreement by opening and closing

his eyes.

Mr Fleggjoy left his position by the well-used mirror and walked over and stood above his little charge. 'You, who take all your sustenance from the 'and of Fleggjoy, do not see fit to appear for a day or two. And to what do I put down this gap in communication, my fine fellow? 'ave you found a more splendid and more loving 'ousehold to get your victuals from, eh?' Mr Fleggjoy often found it necessary to talk to Dickens as though he were an erring junior clerk rather than an erring cat. 'So, my little fellow, you will find this pleasant morning that I am none too pleased with the sight of you, especially as I am the sole provider of all your well-being.'

Often Dickens would leave the comfort of the Fleggjoy household and make his way through back streets and alleys in search of the busy mouse and scurrying rat. In the best traditions of cat logic, a few nights away from creature comforts seemed essential to him.

At this moment, Mr Fleggjoy's diatribe to Dickens on his ingratitude was interrupted. Just then the mistress stuck her head around the door and, with a series of squeaks, encouraged her husband to ' 'op along quick'.

Mr Fleggjoy wagged another finger at the family pet, pronounced some biblical profundity about gratitude, and then left. The erring Dickens took the opportunity to jump on to a sofa and fall into a deep, comfortable sleep. After two nights bivouacking, he needed a little more than a cat nap. And there in the comfort of the Fleggjoy drawing room with its abundance of chairs, its lyrical arrangements of curtains and carpets, and the poetic array of wallpaper and pictures, he could feel entirely at his ease. Sunshine streamed through the window as Dickens reposed in this realm of plenty.

Soon after the cat fell deeply asleep, the Fleggjoy carriage left Periodic Square with Mr and Mrs Fleggjoy giving the odd regal wave to friend, neighbour and acquaintance. In their lustrous black-lacquered carriage, they looked every bit the 'elevated' couple.

Passing through the streets of London was indeed a rude

affair. Street traders, carriers, porters, piemen and all the panoply of low street life were much in evidence. And many of these simple people felt obliged to comment on or to offer their wares to the occupants of the large, shiny carriage: 'A lovely bookette for the lady, sir? For that 'andsome pile of humanity beside yer? If she's not yer wife, sir, we're not telling!' It was not unlike swatting flies on a hot night in the Orient, and Mr and Mrs Fleggjoy did their best to keep up their regal pretensions.

Thus the Fleggjoys had to run the gauntlet if they wished to make the journey out. To the privileged couple, it was a social necessity, for in passing through the streets in their fine carriage, looking for all the world like a movable feast of plenty, were they not an encouragement to the many? Was it not like saying to all these people, 'Look! You, too, can climb from the mire of social indifference! Here sits the son of a drayman and the daughter of a laundress! Secure in the comforts of good investment, brought about by hard work and application!'

So the Fleggjoys took the barbs and the insults as a necessary part of being socially elevated. It was the least they could do, to be a living manifestation of what could be achieved in England, through hard work, in the second year of Victoria's reign.

6
Further
Better Times

It was the night before Christmas and Dickens sat by the fire in the drawing room observing the antics of festive preparation. Mr Fleggjoy was overseeing the arrival of a table from the breakfast room, carefully instructing Jenks and Tetley in the finer points of carrying furniture without damaging the paintwork.

'There, a little to the left, now to the right, yes, a little lower, now up a bit.' To Mr Fleggjoy, the task required military precision, and like so many people who knew not the first thing about the Relief of Salamanca, he believed he knew a thing or two about moving furniture.

'There, just lower it a bit. Good.' The intense concentration soon brought beads of sweat to the brows of the servants and their overseer, and when finally they had manhandled the large oaken table into place, they drew a collective sigh of intense relief.

'Well done, men,' said the overseer. 'Now just the chairs and we will 'ave completed our task.' The two servants uniformly doffed imaginary hats and went off to the breakfast room to bring in the chairs as Mr Fleggjoy stood and surveyed the positioning of the table.

Every year the very same thing happened. On the night before Christmas, all manner of furniture needed to be moved about, for on the morrow a horde of relatives, near relatives, business colleagues and, it was to be hoped, a few prominent neighbours would join the Fleggjoys for a yuletide 'At Home'. Some, of course, would stay on for dinner, but others would just drop in for a drink and a taste from the vast array of comestibles that would be scattered on tables small and large throughout the drawing room.

Although to all intents and purposes Mr Fleggjoy's supervision of his underlings was not entirely necessary, he was obliged to play his role. Mrs Fleggjoy, in a panic in the kitchen overseeing the overseeing of the preparations, insisted on her husband's presence at the rearrangement. 'Idle 'ands, sir, idle 'ands, while others labour. Why, it is a contempt.' This she had said in the kitchen, wagging a large wooden spoon in Mr Fleggjoy's direction. 'I will not 'ave idle hands when the world is slaving, sir, so you go and prove your use.'

But the way in which Mrs Fleggjoy said this made it sound unlike bald censure. It was, in a strange sort of way, Mr Fleggjoy thought, like playing games. For the moment, Mrs Fleggjoy was cast in the role of hard-working housewife. And he, the willing but silly husband, must bow to her momentary disguise of housewifely tyrant.

Dickens, as with all cats, of course, was immaterial to the events and took only a passing interest in them. Deep within his memory, he may well have remembered a similar event the previous year, but the purpose in rearranging things and with such heartfelt agonies could not be fathomed by the cat, and he was as content as always merely to observe.

Now Mr Fleggjoy set about checking that all was in order. A list that he carried around in his head was inwardly ticked off and soon exhausted, and with it Mr Fleggjoy. Once the staff had been directed back to their normal labours, he collapsed into his armchair and congratulated himself on another fine display of his organizational skills. Sipping from a small glass of port, he had no trouble convincing himself that he deserved a rest from his trying labours.

Dickens, well and truly curled up into the proverbial ball, drew intense satisfaction (for the moment at least) from the fact that he was not out in the ice and snow of Periodic

Square. Disporting himself before the fire was one of his ideas of heaven, and though this form of heaven was experienced often by the Fleggjoy cat, it never lost its attraction.

By the by, Mrs Fleggjoy felt compelled to check the overseeing of her husband, who on such matters she only trusted so far. Mr Fleggjoy might be a powerhouse in the matters of bonds and investments, but around the house he was little better than Dickens in the efficacy of his actions. Predictably, when she arrived in the drawing room, Mrs Fleggjoy found reasons to rearrange the odd chair here or a small table there. She fussed about this and fussed about that as Mr Fleggjoy sat in his armchair relishing the fine old port that Mr Delloyt himself had personally recommended.

'You are but a novice at such things, sir,' declared Mrs Fleggjoy. 'A complete and utter novice,' she repeated as she puffed up a few rather deflated cushions.

But this, we must grasp, was not a comment of censure. Each in their own way enjoyed the knowledge that they were expert in certain things and incompetent in others. It pleased them that the division of labour they operated allowed a man to be a complete and bumbling fool in one department and a woman to be a complete and bumbling fool in another. For the division of labour was the greatest of inventions, and Mrs Fleggjoy, in particular, loved to describe her spouse as a 'babe in arms' in matters domestic.

' 'orses for courses, madam, 'orses for courses,' mumbled Mr Fleggjoy as he held up to the light the luxuriant tipple that was his compensation for the debilitating effects of the previous half an hour's work.

Dickens was now asleep, missing the performance that kept Mrs Fleggjoy recommending and then changing and then rechanging, while her husband savoured his respite.

'We 'ave got to get it right, sir,' said Mrs Fleggjoy as she looked at the assembled furniture with the eye of a French empress laying out the designs for her ideal city. 'It ain't enough to go off 'alf cocked, is it, sir?' To which her husband readily agreed. 'And if needs be, I'll stay up all night to get the 'ole place right.'

As Mr Fleggjoy sat, occasionally sipping and occasionally holding up his port to the light, as he had seen other gentlemen do, he could not help but think about the snugness of the world in which he now lived. Outside, snow and inclemency made their unhappy mark on the city, but here within, the large fire, the fine furnishings and glistening lights seemed the perfection of all things, the very backbone of his happiness. To be happy about one's possessions was one thing, but to be happy about the glittering light and the heat thrown from a fire in one's comfortable drawing room was worth all the outward signs of plenty. *Let them (whoever they are) keep their paradings and ostentation*, thought Mr Fleggjoy. *Leave me with the joy of light an' 'eat, of contentment – and an ample bottle of fine old port. Take the rest and do with it as you wish*, he reflected, *but an Englishman is 'appiest in the warmth of 'is 'ouse, in the snugness of 'is drawing room while 'is spouse busies 'erself and the family pet lies before the fire in a state of complete happiness.*

Mr Fleggjoy loved Christmas because it was at such times that one could feel good about the world. It was a time which ignited in his mind the joys of being a Christian in a Christian country at a time of national celebration. And though there were those who were not as fortunate, the present condition of society was the nearest to achievable perfection. *Is it not true*, mused Mr Fleggjoy, now on his favourite subject of self-improvement, *that it is the duty of all to climb out of the mire, as I 'ave done?* Oh, he remembered almost with indignation those who had wasted opportunity and hope in the quaffing of spirits and porter when, in fact, they should have been doing other things more pertinent to the improvement of themselves. But it was the nature of society that those who hugged the bottom of things did so largely because they had turned their backs on bringing themselves on. And to those, Mr Fleggjoy, gentleman, would not spare a thought. *It is all to a purpose*, Mr Fleggjoy reassured himself.

Mrs Fleggjoy, in the meantime, was not thinking of the

social implications of warm fires and the shine of the well-polished table. Her mind was not set to thinking upon the state of prosperity in Olde England and the unique balance of its social structure. She had more mundane things to be concerned with, such as how was it possible to get upwards of twenty people into a room that, though large and plentifully furnished, was not designed to take the generous rears of that amount of humanity in a sitting position? And not only were there these twenty persons, but also at least a half dozen servants to supply them with endless rounds of delicacies and drinks. The solution therefore was a kind of buffet, but not one in which the persons comfortably perched would have to rise off their 'bottoms' – the nearest available servant would supply them where they sat. And all this was to happen from eleven o'clock the following morning.

Having exhausted the already exhausted possibilities of the drawing room, Mrs Fleggjoy went elsewhere to do other things that did not really need doing. But that was the nature of the woman. It was her wont to fuss and fidget reality into whatever shape was felt necessary, and though she was not a born hostess, she had the driving need to feel perfectly happy with the content of her house when she woke of a morning.

Soon the arranging of the arrangements had so tired the poor woman and her spouse that they collapsed into their matrimonial arbour. Within minutes, they were in slumber in their large bedroom in their large house in Periodic Square, while outside the house winds whipped and sprayed the newly fallen snow into small alpine ranges. As Mrs Fleggjoy dreamt of sensible things and Mr Fleggjoy dreamt of worthy things, another fall of snow hung somewhere in the west to deposit itself soon on the vastness of London.

If humans have their 'wonts', so do cats. And if it is the wont of a cat to venture forth in the most inclement weather, we cannot question its motives. Possibly it has to do with the cat's well-honed idea of opposites. Contradiction may be the bread and butter of their lives, and this, in some ways, stops them from becoming soft and ineffectual. Do they need to

venture out in order to appreciate even more the obverse of these conditions, namely the fire in the hearth and the comfortable sofa in front of it?

Mrs Catalyst let the little fellow out, though not without a blessing that he stayed clear of the ice and the snow. 'Good night then, little fellow,' she said, closing the door behind Dickens. 'Don't you go getting yourself all frozen up.' With these words, the night bolts were drawn, the gaslight in the back of the house was extinguished, and Mrs Catalyst took herself off to the comfort of her bed. Slipping between the cold sheets, she could not help but imagine Dickens stalking the icy regions of the night, and thanked God that He had not brought her into the world furred and fourlegged.

Dickens, once outside, looked into the dim Christmas night and mulled over his next move. He would have possibly liked to encounter a nice fat mouse that sought an early extinction, or a long tail with whom he could have a rare game before the inevitable end.

But there were no long tails to greet him. Nor was there another of his own species with whom he might have a bit of fun in the form of a snarl or a fight. No, all there was to greet him was the wind, the snow and the ice. So taking little apparent interest in the white world and the indifferent opportunities presented to him, he nonchalantly set out to walk beyond the confines of Periodic Square, where not a living soul was to be seen.

Having left the square, Dickens now saw the odd stragglers trying to hold their own in the wintry blast. It was the early hours of Christmas morning and a few people still had a mind to cut through the snow to distant hearths. Dickens watched these bravers of the elements with their thick cloak-coats flapping in the unceasing wind. He passed through the snow-filled court-yards of Lincoln's Inn that, during the day, were thronged with bum-bailiffs, clerks, solicitors and legal magicians who could turn black into its opposite in the interest of justice and who knew the top and bottom of a codicil as well as Dickens knew the backbone of an Aberdeen kipper.

Banks of snow had by now made many of the passages and courts impassible. *Not much chance of the kings of rodentry around here*, might have been Dickens' thought as he negotiated the rather difficult geography brought on by the weather.

Even on his most blighted of nights at this most blighted of hours, Dickens encountered little knots of troubled people who huddled in the closes and passages, beyond the enquiring lamps of the peelers. Wispy people with no more blood in their veins than a cockroach did their huddling in cold stairways and doorways, and as Dickens passed, he would often pause and look into the dark recesses. No shadow could hide them from his sharp eye, and though they did not like the eye of anyone to fall upon them, Dickens' two green ones caused them no consternation.

Having negotiated the narrows of Lincoln's Inn, Dickens came out into the maze of little passages and alleys that were the object of his journey. Dickens the hunter continued his odyssey with optimistic determination, even in these evil conditions.

But then, was life simply the pursuit of the long tail? Was life just a long and eventful chase, a dash after, a catching up with, a quick dispatch following a seemingly interminable game? Was this the purpose of life? one asks oneself. If it were, was it this that drove him out from the comfort of Fleggjoyiana?

No one has ever answered these questions, in the same way that no one has ever come back from the dead to tell us what it is like. No one even in this age of plenty could tell you in all honesty that they knew the machinations of the cat. A cat who, as Mrs Fleggjoy once commented, was a cat was a cat was a cat.

When he arrived at Dumpling Passage, Dickens took up his position on the wall at the end of the passage, which allowed him a good view. Sitting, he looked down at the snow-strewn passage and looked up at the little houses. Few lights could be seen. Little noise could be heard. Even Dumpling Passage seemed to have been subdued by inclemency.

No, there is an as yet unwritten law that a cat will often venture to the extremities of things simply to look around and then wander back again. It is a law that is probably as old as catdom itself. And this night, as the world was sensibly wrapped up in its bed, or huddling in alleys and doorways, Dickens sat on the wall of his choosing and looked down at the blighted expanses of a snow-laden world. Possibly on many other walls in many other parts of the capital other cats were doing the same. But Dickens, a cat transmogrified from penury to plenty, was an especial cat. And why he still chose to explore the cold night when the vermin were well hidden in culvert and drain, we shall never know.

After some while on the wall, Dickens left his seat and took the route back to Periodic Square.

Another night, another day.

7
The
Presentiment

Down, down into the quagmire of frowsy and foul-smelling humanity, to the bottom of the unfit dregs of the realm, down deeper than poverty, to disorder and dishonour, to the cesspit of life, the cemetery of hope and respectability. Down to the labyrinth of ugliness. And once down, never, never to rise again ...

Mr Fleggjoy woke with a start, covered in a terrible and uncomfortable sweat. He gulped the air, now free of his purgatorial dream.

'Madam!' he called out in alarm in the thin dawn light that crept through the badly drawn curtains and threw some illumination into the otherwise dark room. 'Madam!' he called again. But madam was snoring a tasteless snore and was oblivious to the terror that rang in her husband's gasping voice. 'Mrs Fleggjoy!' he tried but to no avail. 'Lulucia!' he attempted, but this went equally unacknowledged by the contented sleeping form of his mate. 'My treasure!' – but there was little chance of waking his sleeping partner without a thorough good shake, and though he momentarily considered it, he soon put the thought out of his mind. 'Then, madam,' he said to himself, 'if you cannot rouse yourself, then I am truly alone.'

Drawing back the covers, he sat up in bed and felt the dampness on his forehead. 'Oh, madam, I have been sent to 'ell and back, and I was there alone, with not a soul to save me!' He certainly was alone at this hour, filled with foreboding from his night's terror. 'Oh, madam, when I need you most, you snore like a drunken matelot.' This was, of course, an unkind observation to make, especially as his sleeping wife could not be blamed for being in deep slumber at this early-dawn hour and, being a loving man, Mr Fleggjoy immediately apologised to her sleeping bulk.

Unsteadily he got out of bed and tried to rid himself of the dregs of his dream. By breathing in deeply and shaking his head with a certain vigour, he managed to induce some sense into his troubled mind. From the small table by the bed, which held an array of tablets and night lotions, he took his pocket watch and, opening it, endeavoured to see the time. *(Oh time! time! that eats away at opportunity!)* Unable to make out the exact position of the hands he gingerly crept to the window, for now that he was more awake, he was desirous not to rouse the sleeping woman with whom he shared most of life's hopes and anxieties.

At the window, the light showed that it was just before the hour of five. Below, in Periodic Square, not a soul could alleviate Mr Fleggjoy's sense of isolation. Even the early morning twitter of birds could not drive from him his deep sense of being the only person at that moment awake and in the throes of some deep crisis. *Perhaps*, he thought, *there are others who at this moment are also standing by windows troubled by the dreams of collapse and failure ...*

At the thought of others in other houses in the square his mind alighted on the image of Mr and Mrs Utterpout lying abed. He imagined, though he had never seen it, their large bedroom with the contented couple in some primaeval four-poster, snoring and oblivious to the fact that, across the square, their friend and financial adviser had been driven from the warmth of his bed to stand by the window. *Would they*, he thought, *leave their comfortable, warm bed to cheer me up?*

But such musings, he decided, were foolish. With as much silence as he could manage, he pulled on his dressing gown and opened the large bedroom door, which emitted a creak so loud that it could have woken a hanged man. But no, Mrs Fleggjoy remained hibernative and in the arms of Morpheus.

49

Mr Fleggjoy, having passed through the door, now closed it behind him, making a mental note that he would have to get its hinges oiled as soon as possible.

Creeping across the landing, he made his way down the stairs to the ground floor and, having arrived there without incident, he went down another flight to the basement. To feel the warmth of the banked-up kitchen fire was his intention and, sure enough, once through the kitchen door this was what he encountered. The overnight fire was to him like the light of a beacon to a lost mariner. 'Oh, my beauty,' he said as though he were addressing a living thing. Standing before the fire, he was quickly revived and the night's terror began to slip from him.

He pulled up a chair and sat looking deep into the flickering coals. 'Oh, what a night I 'ave 'ad,' he whispered, 'the kind of night I would not wish on anyone. Full of ugliness and pain. Full of failure and falling. Oh, the very thought makes me 'eart quiver.'

He sat for a few minutes talking to the fire, and then, taking up a poker, he decided to enliven it. The fire was soon crackling away, throwing out even more life-reviving warmth on to the troubled man who sat before it. Mr Fleggjoy tried to put from his mind once and for all the presentiment of imminent disaster. He would, he decided, think of the good things of life rather than the possibility that all the plenty that he now experienced was about to be taken from him. *Why, he told himself, it was stupid even to think of it. For there is no evidence that my prosperity is in any way questionable, what with the strength of my investments and my position as partner in the 'old firm'.*

But something still niggled at his sense of well-being. Mr Delloyt (whom he trusted implicitly) seemed always too busy to tie up the final little details as monies moved hither and thither. This disturbed Mr Fleggjoy, who was a man given to the keeping of copious accounts and the copious giving of receipts. But Mr Delloyt had of late avoided the tallying up of numerous things, and as he was the senior partner, Mr Fleggjoy was not in a position to insist. But a nagging feeling that he must

address himself to Mr Delloyt's eccentric accounting system still held sway in his mind.

But, Mr Fleggjoy thought to himself, *Mr Delloyt is in 'is own way the model of 'onesty and efficiency.* He would trust him with his life and, in some respects, he already had.

Mr Fleggjoy's musings were soon interrupted by a noise coming from outside. Jettisoning speculation from his mind, he sat up and listened. Sure enough, beyond the door were the sounds of whining and scratching. And as soon as Mr Fleggjoy realized who the perpetrator of these sounds was, his face lit up.

He drew back the great bolts of the solid oaken kitchen door and opened it to the little fellow who sat waiting. 'Oh, my dear chap, 'ow fortuitous, 'ow splendidly fortuitous.'

Dickens looked up at his master, gave a *miaow* in a minor key and then walked past him into the kitchen. Once inside, he surveyed his bowl and, on seeing nothing there, looked up at his provider.

'All right, you little fiend,' said his provider, 'let's see what we can get for you.' Mr Fleggjoy opened the larder, and on seeing a fine piece of fish, he offered it to his hungry little charge. Dickens made short shrift of it while his master looked on contentedly. 'You carry on, my little chap,' said Mr Fleggjoy. 'It's your right as a greedy little fellow to be fed on demand. Pity that my world is not as simple as yours. But it is not and there's not an awful lot we can do about it.'

When he had finished his meal, Dickens was scooped up by Mr Fleggjoy. Master and cat sat in the chair before the fire in a mood of contentment. Mr Fleggjoy stroked his little companion and told him about his dream and its dreadful ramifications.

'Oh, my little fellow, if only you knew the night I've 'ad. An inferno would 'ave been more tolerable than what I 'ave been through tonight.'

Dickens looked up occasionally at the man who was telling him a story while, at the same time, stroking him firmly. Dickens was in his element: he had had an adventurous night out, had had a good fill, and was now being cosseted. Although he might have preferred silence to the droning voice of his provider, he showed no obvious signs of this. *As far as I am concerned* (might have been his reasoning), *you have to take the rough with the smooth.* And, if being talked to was the worst of the arrangement, then he had at least a full belly, the heat from the fire and the continual stroking as compensation for the mutterings of his troubled master.

They sat like this until some time after six, when Mrs Catalyst came into the kitchen to find master and cat asleep in the chair.

It had been a bad night, but thank goodness, it was now over.

8

The Fall
of
The House of Fleggjoy

Catastrophes tend by their very nature to be sudden, and the fall of the house of Fleggjoy was no different. There are often hidden signs that the sharp-eyed few might pick up, but one would have had to have been an acute observer to have noticed the truth behind the fabric with regard to the Fleggjoy establishment. There had been no external manifestations of decline or imminent collapse; the Fleggjoys had seemed as prosperous as ever, going about their lives of collecting bric-a-brac and experiences as a jackdaw might accumulate shiny objects for its nest.

No, on this day, morning came like any other, but in truth there was calamity hidden under the garb of life's mundanity. And as befits our story of the house of Fleggjoy, Dickens was present at the arrival of the harbingers of the catastrophe to come.

If cats were equipped with other than the sensory organs of little murderers of the undergrowth, they might notice such things as the arrival of men in the strange uniform of the constabulary. Cats, though, would not therefore register any interest even in the livery of officialdom. Thus, early on the morning that Dickens saw two peelers and an accompanying fellow dressed in street clothes standing outside the Fleggjoy establishment, he was no more interested in them than he would be in the elegant bulging skirts of a society hostess. As the three 'gentlemen' eyed and then approached the house, his mind was more likely engrossed in what he would find in his bowl once he gained access.

As one man knocked on the door and then awaited a response, Dickens crossed the road and expectantly joined the visitors. One of the constables happened to notice Dickens and was about to bend down and stroke him when something warned him against it. Could it have been the thought that such an action might be seen as fraternizing with the enemy? (The enemy being all wrongdoers, and the particular wrongdoers in this case being the Fleggjoys.)

Though the knocking had boomed through the house, there was no answer, and a second even heavier one had to be applied to the glistening Fleggjoy knocker. This would have certainly woken the prophets from their sleep and therefore had the intended effect. The sound of the great night bolts being pulled back was heard, followed by the door being opened by an irate Mrs Catalyst who, simply by her scowl, suggested that seven o'clock of a morning was not a respectable hour to call on a respectable house.

But Mrs Catalyst's accusative grimace soon turned from censure to astonishment. Opening the door wide, she immediately realized with the wisdom of the honest that the three visitors were not calling to announce that another fine late spring day had commenced. Rather, Mrs Catalyst observed, something must be amiss for such an early morning visitation to take place.

'G'morning,' replied the housekeeper. 'And what can I do for you, sir?'

'This is, I believe, the house of Mr Fleggjoy?' said the detective without directly answering Mrs Catalyst's question.

'It is, sir,' replied the anxious woman. 'Mr Falstaff Fleggjoy that is, gentlemen.'

'Quite, quite,' replied the detective, not surprised that he had arrived at the right address. 'I am a police officer, and these are two police constables.' The detective now cleared an imaginary obstruction from his throat, and proceeded to ask if he could see Mr Fleggjoy, adding 'if that was at all possible'. This addition was, of course, an unnecessary pleasantry because, whether it were possible or not, he *would* see Mr Fleggjoy.

Dickens had not waited for the introductions. He had shot through the forest of legs and was soon making his way down the basement stairs to the kitchen. While he badgered Cook Bleery for what was his due, the detective entered the house, but not before he had directed the two constables to stand guard outside, one by the front door and the other by the mews corner. But this was only a formal precaution. Gentlemen like Mr Fleggjoy did not normally do a runner.

Once inside the house, the police officer, who had removed his hat, was directed into the small anteroom and told to wait for a moment while the master was informed of his presence. Mrs Catalyst then went to the breakfast room to inform Mr Fleggjoy of the unexpected visitors. As she traversed the short distance, she did all she could to restore her composure.

Mr Fleggjoy sat hunched over his repast of a lightly boiled egg, reading the *Morning Despatch* with the dedication of a man who took an interest in all matters of the contemporary world. His unsuspecting posture was about to be disturbed, and inwardly Mrs Catalyst felt unhappy at playing the part of the disturber.

Standing beside her master and, leaning slightly, Mrs Catalyst said with as much lightness as she could muster, 'There is a gentleman to see you, sir.' However, the detectable emphasis in her voice betrayed her opinion that the 'gentleman' probably was not, in fact, any such thing. But whatever the social status of the man in the small anteroom, he was certainly calling at a very peculiar hour.

Mr Fleggjoy pulled his eyes away from the newspaper and looked up at Mrs Catalyst with a certain disbelief. 'Are you saying, Mrs Catalyst, that we 'ave a visitor at this hour?' An hour, he might have added, when all decent people were either still in their beds, or at their ablutions, or, if a dedicated early riser like himself, at their breakfast tables. But nobody who

56

could call himself a gentleman would be up and about at this hour.

'Yes, sir,' said Mrs Catalyst in reply. Then she lowered her eyes in order not to see the terror in her master's at the completion of her message: 'He is, sir, a police officer.' Sure enough, if Mrs Catalyst had looked up at that moment, she would have seen the fear and the confusion of a man who, though believing himself entirely innocent of all things, was not likely to enjoy a visit from the constabulary at this or any hour.

Mr Fleggjoy stood and walked out into the hall without asking further information from his housekeeper. He went directly into the anteroom, closing the door softly behind him.

While events unfolded upstairs, Dickens stood sentry by his bowl and wondered when Cook Bleery would respond to his overtures for service. His insistence did not, however, draw the cook from her work, for now was one of the most busy times of the day. She ignored the rubbing and the *miaowing* as she rushed around to prepare the breakfast of the mistress who would at any minute be rising from her slumbers.

Eventually Cook Bleery did break off from her endeavours and gave the ravenous fellow the morsels that she had kept for him on the larder slab: 'There now, a little waiting gives a good edge to the appetite.'

Cook Bleery was laying out the mistress's tray when Mrs Catalyst appeared in the kitchen with the look of a Protestant who had narrowly escaped the Inquisition. But Cook was not in one of her more observant moods, and Mrs Catalyst had to make a whole series of swooning sighs before she was noticed by her fellow-worker. When Cook finally realised that there was something troubling Mrs Catalyst, she immediately abandoned her tray-laying and became, for the moment, 'all ears'.

'Mrs Catalyst,' asked the cook, 'what is it that troubles you this morning?' Mrs Catalyst did a spin, not unlike a graceless pirouette, and then, putting her hands to her face, fell into Cook's chair. This, under normal circumstances, would have warranted a sharp cry of protest, but this morning Mrs Catalyst's distress seemed of such magnitude that even the proprietorial inclinations of the cook were temporarily suspended.

'Oh, Cook, Cook,' dramatically moaned the distressed housekeeper, now sitting in the chair of the captain of the kitchen. 'Cook, if you'd only seen what I seen.' In the minds of women like Cook Bleery, such utterings would normally have conjured up such images as a master coming out of a female servant's room in a state of undress. But in the Fleggjoy household, such 'goings on' never went on, so Cook Bleery was even more interested in what Mrs Catalyst had actually seen.

'And what, pray, is it that you saw?' asked the cook in a state of instant and total fascination.

Mrs Catalyst now conspiratorially lent forward and, in doing so, gestured for the cook to come as close as she could. Almost into the ear of the other woman, Mrs Catalyst told her of the arrival of a special kind of visitor who was not about to enquire after the health of the master. In short, she told Cook Bleery of the police officer, adding for flavour her distinct impression that Mr Fleggjoy seemed to become instantly upset, almost as though he already knew the purpose of the visit.

The effect on Cook Bleery was all that Mrs Catalyst could have wished for. For a moment, she looked every bit as though she had been struck by a badly waved frying pan, causing her to become unsteady at the knees. Unfortunately for Cook Bleery her own chair was already occupied, so she had to sink into the chair of the kitchen maid, who luckily was at that moment at Covent Garden purchasing watercress for the evening meal's soup.

The two women sat looking at each other with intensity and feeling, unspoken words mixed with shock and some degree of excitement. And if they had voiced their fears it would probably have been along the lines that there was 'no smoke without fire'. And though Mr Fleggjoy had been a good master, his rise from indifference to prosperity had been, in the opinion of the two women, somewhat too rapid – something they were to reflect upon soon afterwards. But for the moment, all they could do was sit and look at each other and wonder whether or not they were at the scene of a very bad scorching or a conflagration.

Having finished his morsels and lapped some milk from his other bowl, Dickens surveyed the scene. Above him at the kitchen table, all labour, which had been so intense a few minutes before, had ceased as Mrs Catalyst and Cook Bleery whispered their suspicions to each other. Mrs Catalyst volunteered the idea that 'they' normally called on people first thing in the morning in order to apprehend them and stop them from going off to other parts. Such observations Mrs Catalyst quickly qualified with the rider that, although this was indeed what happened in many instances, it was not likely in the case presently under discussion.

Dickens, though, did not waste a moment in a kitchen full not with the busy hands of labour but with the busy speculations of the two women. So while they mused upon whether Mr Fleggjoy was guilty or innocent of everything from homicide to indecent exposure, Dickens climbed the basement stairs up to the front hall and waited to gain entry into the drawing room, where, in imitation of social etiquette, Mr Fleggjoy had taken the detective from the small anteroom. And while Dickens sat waiting for entry, his master took a few turns on the carpet before the unlit fireplace.

'But this is impossible, officer,' said Mr Fleggjoy. 'Slaughterfoot, Cockensie & Delloyt 'ave always been most strict about matters of clients' monies.'

At this, the detective cleared another imaginary stoppage in his throat. 'Are you not forgetting something, Mr Fleggjoy?' he said with a certain look of pleasure on his face. 'Are you not forgetting, sir, that we are dealing with, if I might remind you, Slaughterfoot, Cockensie, Delloyt & Fleggjoy?'

'Yes, of course,' came the limp reply.

The very suggestion that the 'firm' was in any way involved in the nefarious business of depriving clients of their monies elicited the kind of response from Mr Fleggjoy that one might expect from a man who believed wholeheartedly in the integrity of those with whom he worked. He knew for certain that he had, in all his years, not so much as turned a dishonest farthing. And as for Mr Delloyt, why the very thought was unimaginable.

'Are you saying, sir,' began the detective again after a few moments of dramatic pause, 'that you know nothing of the monies that have disappeared from at least five of your clients' accounts?'

'I know most of our clients, officer,' said Mr Fleggjoy with as much emphasis as he could muster, 'but I know of nothing under'and.' To Mr Fleggjoy, this last sentence should have put paid to any suggestion of dishonesty, but unfortunately the police officer viewed things differently.

'Then are you saying, sir, that not only were you not party to any of this calumny but that you knew nothing about it?'

The point of asking the same question in a different way was entirely lost on Mr Fleggjoy, but as dramatic emphasis was obviously called for, he would oblige. He stopped wringing his hands and ceased pacing across the carpet. With the best effect he could muster, he pushed his arms behind his back and stood up as straight as his years and indifferent physique would allow. Now fully erect, relatively speaking, and with the demeanour of a successful publican in his dressing gown, he laid his integrity formally before the visiting investigator.

'Sir: I am not and never 'ave been party to any type of crime in any shape or form. I 'ave zealously cared for the interests of those whose monies I 'ave been asked to 'andle and, with equal zealousness, have overseen the monies that the company 'as also 'andled. So even if I 'ave not been directly responsible for the monies, I 'ave, in the interest of the company, seen that all transactions 'ave been carried out in the most proper manner.'

At this he pushed out his bulging middle, seeming to gain at least an inch in height in the process. It had been a fine speech. The problem was that, in his rush to protect the integrity of the company, he was putting himself in the position to take all the blame. He was the company, and anything untoward with regard to the company's business was the

responsibility of him, Falstaff Fleggjoy, gentleman and partner.

This, though, was far from true. In all matters, Mr Delloyt had had a free hand. But Fleggjoy was so convinced of the honesty and integrity of the company and of his partner that he was prepared to put his head on the block in their defence.

It was the detective's turn to pace across the carpet before the unlit fire while Mr Fleggjoy took a seat. For a moment, a puzzled silence fell between them while the detective walked, hands folded behind him, back and forth. Stopping, as if something profound had risen to the surface of his mind, he turned and looked hard at Mr Fleggjoy.

'Who, sir, are the partners of your firm?' Fleggjoy hesitated before replying, and when his reply came, it was as limp as any spent daffodil. 'The partnership is Mr Delloyt and myself. Mr Cockensie sold up to Mr Delloyt and myself one year ago. Mr Slaughterfoot is now deceased, but his wife takes a share of the profits.' He had said enough. The police officer had confirmed something that he had already known: that the partnership in its most active sense comprised Mr Delloyt and Mr Fleggjoy. Having interviewed the *real* gentleman, Mr Delloyt, he was now convinced that the true culprit was the man standing before him.

Dickens, sitting in the hall outside, was not party to this discussion between his master and his master's inquisitor. He sat and licked himself for a few minutes before turning and going through the open door of the breakfast room, a room that he was not particularly partial to but which was better than a poke in the eye with a burnt stick. For whereas the drawing room looked over the busy and active square, the breakfast room looked over the relative quiet of the garden.

This morning Dickens would have to settle for second best. Once in the room, he climbed on to the windowsill and gazed out at the vast openness of the lawn where the odd pigeon was parading and celebrating its rather simple existence. He positioned himself in the window and watched with indifference. To him, excitement meant the undergrowth, and he had therefore no time for the openness of the lawn.

Today, however, something rather interesting was happening in the garden. He noticed a marmalade under a tree in the traditional posture of the stalking cat. And to top it all, not a few feet from the marmalade a fat, distracted wood pigeon seemed lost in contemplation. Dickens pricked his ears and narrowed his eyes as he watched the unfolding drama. With the stealth of a committed and practised killer, the marmalade crept slowly forward. The pigeon, unaware of what was happening over its shoulder, carried on with its reflections. Stealthily the cat moved closer and was now within pouncing distance.

The tension was electric. Sitting in the window, Dickens was so wrapped up in the scene below him that he did not hear the rather noisy stirrings in the hall, where Mrs Fleggjoy had arrived from the marital bedroom just as her husband was about to come and tell her that a police officer had called and had asked Mr Fleggjoy to accompany him back to the police station. Mrs Fleggjoy, fresh from slumber, protested sleepily but loudly.

Dickens, meanwhile, was busy watching the climax of the drama between the marmalade and the pigeon. Suddenly the bird made a lame and late attempt to find out what was occurring over its shoulder. And at that moment, the marmalade launched itself in a vicious leap of death. The cat dug its claws into the bird with all the confidence of an animal certain of its catch. Loud squawks and flapping wings did nothing to free the pigeon, and though it continued to protest, it was well and truly caught.

'What means all this?' demanded Mrs Fleggjoy as she pushed past her husband, who was standing in the drawing room doorway, and confronted the police officer. Fleggjoy came back into the room and, closing the door behind him, tried to give his spouse a thumbnail sketch of what had transpired.

'Are you accusing this man, my husband . . . ?' Her voice trailed off into incomprehension, Mrs Fleggjoy unable to consider that her husband was capable of even the mildest of transgressions. 'But, sir,' she finally said to both parties, 'this cannot be true.'

'It cannot be and is not,' emphasized her husband, but the response from his inquisitor was only a faint shrug of the shoulders and the retrieval of his hat from the small table.

Mrs Fleggjoy watched with increasing confusion as Mr Fleggjoy went up to dress while the detective went out to tell his two accomplices that they would be leaving shortly and that one of them should hail a cab.

Dickens sat and watched the marmalade reduce the pigeon to little more than a feather duster and then retire into the bushes that fringed the lawn. Once the drama had passed, Dickens got down from the windowsill and settled on a chair for the duration of the morning. In the meantime, Mr Fleggjoy went off with the detective and his assistants, while Mrs Fleggjoy returned to her room to weep and pace the floor.

Later that day, a message was brought to the house that, pending his trial, Mr Fleggjoy was to be committed to Newgate as a common criminal, and his assets were to be frozen until it was established which monies were lawfully his and which were not.

Before going to bed that night, Mrs Fleggjoy took a heavy sleeping draught to block out the events of the day. Dickens did his normal rounds. But he was the only member of the Fleggjoy household that did not see the long shadow that was, even then, engulfing them.

9
Bad Times

To fall is one thing, but to be seen to fall by one's neighbours is distinctly uncomfortable to all who live in the bounteous world of the higher echelons.

Dickens had spent the night in the garden in the centre of Periodic Square among the luxuriant undergrowth. Having sated his appetite for murder, and as it was now his intention to satisfy other appetites in the Fleggjoy kitchen, he came out on to the wide, early-morning pavement and looked up and down the road for someone who, like himself, was about to seek entrance to No. 17. A few unimportant human beings passed the door but without presuming to knock. Dickens might have already made up his mind to seek access through the back when, down the street, he spied someone who might act as a 'key' to the Fleggjoy door.

The figure he recognized had previously worn the hat of many dead birds. Now bare-headed, she was clad in the simplest of attire. Gone were all the flowing antique skirts with a superabundance of hem. And gone also was the former appearance of unhappy crisis. Her firmness of step, aided by her equally firm wielding of her walking stick, was the opposite of the hesitance with which she had approached No. 17 all those afternoons ago when she had wished to see the male Fleggjoy on matters both pressing and grave. Dickens crossed over and awaited the arrival of the social titan with great interest. Already his stomach was preparing for a feast of

Aldeburgh sprats or the large flat pleasures of an Aberdeen kipper.

As Mrs Caselot Monkhaven Utterpout arrived at the mews corner, a large cart drew level with No. 17. Neither Mrs Utterpout nor the expectant Dickens paid much attention to the vehicle, which held three seated men as well as the driver.

'That's it, Charley,' said one to another.

'Right yer are,' replied the driver as he halted the great drayhorse outside the Fleggjoy house.

By this time Mrs Utterpout had arrived at the front door in a state of undiminished aggression. Dickens had taken up his 'I am about to enter' posture, assured now of an imminent feast. Mrs Utterpout, though, had other ideas for Dickens and, with one quick swing of her walking stick, whacked the unsuspecting cat in his nether regions.

'Off you go, you scabrous thing!' she screeched and would have taken another whack if Dickens had not anticipated her next move. 'Off you go, you dirty vermin,' she added as the cat quickly vacated the scene. And then, turning, she noticed that she was not entirely alone outside No. 17.

'Mrs Fleggjoy?' enquired a man in a rough suit and a hat, who seemed to be the captain of the team now gathering on the pavement.

' "Mrs Fleggjoy"?' screamed the social titan. ' "Mrs Fleggjoy"?' The tone of her voice did more to tell the man than all the explanations in the world that not only was this woman not Mrs Fleggjoy but the very idea was quite abhorrent to her. Then, giving the leader of the troupe no time to gather a reply together, she turned her own inquisitorial skills on to her inquisitor. 'And what, sir, is your business with the Fleggjoys?'

'Ah, madam,' said the man, subdued by the sharpness of the woman's tone, 'that is between . . . ' His voice trailed off as Mrs Utterpout turned, having noticed the three other men who all wore the distinctive long leather aprons of the removers' profession.

'Moving?' enquired Mrs Utterpout without the slightest

66

diminution of aggression in her voice.

The man with the suit tipped his hat and, realizing that he stood no chance of getting any further with the angry social titan, politely stepped aside from her and knocked loudly on the Fleggjoy's door.

If Mrs Utterpout could formerly have been described as angry, now she became volcanic. As soon as the door was opened by a polite Mary, the raging woman pushed the maid out of the way and rushed into the hall. 'Fleggjoy!' she screamed. 'Fleggjoy! Where are you, you *thief!*'

The four men, having entered the house, gingerly walked past Mrs Utterpout. While the demented woman had decided not to stand on ceremony, the four men had meekly agreed to wait in the drawing room for the arrival of Mrs Fleggjoy, who, Mary said, would join them shortly.

When the object of her anger did not appear, Mrs Utterpout turned and vented her spleen on young Mary, who was somewhat overwhelmed by it all.

'Where is that crook, your master, girl?' demanded the still boiling and bubbling woman.

'He is, madam,' replied the instantly terrified girl, 'not 'ere, madam.'

'Not here? Not here?' came the outraged reply.

Mary was saved from an even uglier manifestation of volcanic anger by the arrival of Mrs Fleggjoy, who slowly and unsurely descended the stairs looking not unlike a Christian martyr, trepidation and fear written in every crevice of the female Fleggjoy face.

'Agh!' Mrs Utterpout screeched. 'The other half of the criminal partnership!'

'Madam,' tried Mrs Fleggjoy in a state of steady and increasing fear, 'I trust ... '

'Trust? I trust nothing, woman,' came the reply. 'And particularly I do not trust your husband Fleggjoy.'

Mary went into the drawing room to tell the men that Mrs Fleggjoy would be delayed for a minute, and then, picking up her skirts, she rushed down into the basement to tell Mrs

67

Catalyst in the kitchen of the events taking place in the front hall at that very moment.

Dickens had decided after all to seek the back entrance. Now he stood above his bowl of prime Aldeburgh sprats, looking no worse for his rough treatment by the prominent neighbour, while the cook told him that it was possibly the last decent meal he would get this side of Judgement Day and that he should savour every morsel. Cook Bleery was herself convinced that the Fleggjoy's troubles were all the work of some almighty power that takes up and throws down unfortunates with the indifference of a gardener throwing away last year's spent annuals.

'There is a holy logic in everything, Mrs Catalyst,' she was saying to the housekeeper when Mary burst in to tell of the scene in the front hall.

'I'm sure you're right,' managed Mrs Catalyst before she left to follow Mary, 'a terrible logic.'

Dickens, having finished the main part of his meal, refreshed himself from the generous bowl of milk. 'And that, my little fellow, may be the end of the milk of human kindness,' said Cook Bleery. 'The world has turned agin us, lad, and there's not an ounce of tripe you can do about it.' But Dickens' last meal at No. 17 Periodic Square was, in his own terms of reference, uneventful. And thus, when he had finished, he sought an exit through the kitchen door, with which he was dutifully supplied by the oracle of doom.

Mrs Catalyst came upon the ugly sight of her employer virtually in tears before the social titan.

'Your husband in Newgate prison?' bawled the volcanic neighbour in the worst sort of rhetoric heard by either Mrs Fleggjoy or her housekeeper in all their years on earth. 'A common criminal?' carried on the bawler without a reduction in histrionics.

'Yes, Mrs Utterpout,' said the troubled wife.

Mrs Catalyst now joined the fray with the dedication of a Blücher rescuing a forlorn Wellington. And though it was disrespectful in the manner in which it came out, it none the less stemmed the ugly tide of invective from the prominent neighbour.

'And what is all *this?*' screamed the housekeeper with the lungs of a generously proportioned Neopolitan opera singer. Mrs Utterpout's bellow and bawl were quickly established as piffling beside Mrs Catalyst, who rapidly created the impression in the former that she had met her nemesis. The housekeeper, having halted the tirade, now turned on Mrs Utterpout and demanded to know who had invited her to cross the respectable threshold that she now, by her very presence, was polluting.

Mrs Utterpout, so used to giving but not getting, was not up to taking as good as she had given. Her lower lip quivered and her eyes expanded to the size of saucers. 'W-w-why I simply wished . . .' she stuttered at the bitter sounds of Mrs Catalyst.

The ungenerous flow staunched, Mrs Catalyst crossed her arms and stood sentry by her mistress. For a few moments Mrs Utterpout managed to survive the stare of the angry termagant and then stepped backwards to the door, a withdrawal that she was more than happy to make. Feeling her hand on the door, the once Boadicean warrior gratefully turned the handle and exited quickly, still with a look of grave shock on her well-made countenance.

Mrs Utterpout rushed down the steps of No. 17 as fast as her legs could carry her and towards the sanctuary of her own house. The trauma of her encounter had, for the moment, blotted out the memory of the letter received that very morning which advised the Utterpouts that, due to the fall in share prices, there would be no dividends for the foreseeable future. This news had been a shock, since they had been expecting soon to be in clover, like the Fleggjoy household. But now, of course, there was no more chance of this happening than there was of the pyramids of Egypt turning to blancmange. Once back at the Utterpout household, she would have to tell her husband that Newgate and the bailiffs were the order of the day at the once opulent No. 17.

Mrs Catalyst, peeping through the drawing-room curtains, savoured the luxury of watching the erstwhile warrioress scuffle up the road with the fear of God in her. Then, having got as much satisfaction as she could derive from the sight of the precipitate departure, she returned to her distressed mistress. 'Now you go and sit in the drawing room, Mrs Fleggjoy,' said the thoughtful housekeeper.

'But Mrs Catalyst,' said her mistress, 'the bailiffs are there.'

Mrs Catalyst, having drawn blood, suddenly decided to take upon herself some more of the awkward tasks of the day. She marched into the drawing room and found the four men lolling on the Fleggjoy furniture as though it had already arrived at the bankruptcy sale.

'And what are you lot about?' bellowed the housekeeper. 'Is this the way you behave in the 'ouses of your betters?'

They all jumped to attention, and if Mrs Catalyst had been in some kind of uniform, they would almost certainly have saluted her.

'You are the gov'ner 'ere?' she asked the man in the rough suit and the hat.

'I am, missus,' he said, realizing that any advantage hemay have had – the moral high ground, so to speak – had evaporated with the arrival of Mrs Catalyst.

'Then you shall be so good as to make sure that your men treat this 'ouse with respect while they are 'ere. And that, in your task of taking away possessions, you realize that certain items are to go with the mistress to Marshalsea, and that others are the property of myself and the servants.' The man nodded as if to say that he could not agree with her more.

The four removers now set about their work like locusts stripping a tree in full leafy bloom. Their efficiency was heart-less. The man with the rough suit and the hat walked about the house, pulling at this and that, like a prowling dog seeking a cocking point. Another of the men accompanied him with a sheaf of paper on which he wrote down what his superior told him. 'Five bob,' he might say of a table that once would have cost more than the heathen could earn in twelve months, and then, marking it with a cross of white chalk, went on to the next item. 'A quid,' might be the judgement on another piece of furniture whose original purchase price would have left a working man the poorer by 3 years' wages. And as the white chalked crosses multiplied, the two porters came in and took the pieces away.

Thus the official scavengers, who descend upon the fallen in order to liquidate items at bankruptcy sales, were the added dimension to the Fleggjoy's fall. Of course, such families as were going off to the debtors' prison were allowed to keep certain items, but they never were the cream of the collection; they were the remnants that would not even merit inclusion at a 'knockdown' price and which otherwise might even end up as kindling. However, with these sticks of furniture, fallen families were able to keep up some semblance of respectability wherever they ended up.

Mrs Catalyst returned to the kitchen to report this dreadful new development. Cook Bleery raised her hands and eyes to heaven before continuing to sort into a box all the things in the kitchen that belonged to her.

'This is a terrible day,' said the troubled cook, 'and I would not wish it on the worst of my enemies.' Mrs Catalyst agreed wholeheartedly and went off to oversee the gathering and the marking of Mr and Mrs Falstaff Fleggjoy's worldly possessions.

Mrs Fleggjoy, in a state of great confusion, could find nothing better to do than to sit in the drawing room on a chair that she hoped would be left to her to take to the debtors' prison at Marshalsea. But as soon as she had sat down, the man with the rough suit and the hat came in and, apologizing, marked up the room with the Judas crosses.

'That's a fine chair, madam,' he said, having marked up the rest of the contents of the room. Helping her on to a smaller chair, he marked the one on which she had been sitting and then left to do the same thing elsewhere.

Everything in the room having been cursed with the

chalk mark, except for the rather ugly little chair on which Mrs Fleggjoy was seated, the room was then stripped bare by the two leather-aproned porters, who took no time at all to reduce it to an unfamiliar bareness. Mrs Fleggjoy watched these proceedings indifferently, resigned to the thought that having fallen, there was no further place that her fortunes could plummet. Sitting on the chair, she tried to regain what little equilibrium she could from thoughts of her former days at Dumpling Passage. Those times, in comparison with what she was now living through, had been halcyon. The simple life now beckoned, and she resolved there and then, on the only chair in the bare room, never again to place her security in the lap of fortune.

And that was the only original thought that passed through her mind that morning as her life was stripped and laid bare.

When much of the furniture had been put on the liquidators' waggon, another 'gentleman' arrived, who bore the appearance of an official. Having spoken to the 'vultures', he went into the drawing room to talk softly and in a mock concerned voice to the distraught but silent mistress.

'Madam, I have 'ere,' he said to the almost comatose woman, 'the official documents that will allow you to go to Marshalsea.'

Mrs Fleggjoy looked up at him as though the man had brought a tray of refreshments to her cell in a madhouse. Neither smile nor glint of anger crossed her face; there was only emptiness.

'Madam,' the official began again with artificial delicacy, 'I 'ave 'ere the necessary documents pertaining to your removal to the Marshalsea.' He bent down slightly in order that she could see the papers, but he gained no more of her attention by doing this. Mrs Fleggjoy sat with a wanness that contradicted her bulk. Though physically a solid woman, she seemed at this moment to have become remarkably transparent, in essence a shadow. The official stood above the shadow trying to talk to it, not realizing that you can no more converse with a shadow than you can with a cat.

Mrs Catalyst came once more to the rescue. On entering the drawing room and seeing the man, she became again the bombastic woman of an hour before.

'And, sir,' she said, making the man jump as if his vital areas had suddenly been grabbed from behind, 'and what is it that you require of the mistress?'

'Oh,' said the official, now himself reduced to a shadow of his former grand self, 'I wished you, er, your mistress to sign these papers ... '

Mrs Catalyst rudely interrupted the official at this moment and, grabbing the papers from his hands, was desirous of knowing exactly their content and implication. 'Papers?' she asked as she pulled at them as though she were unwrapping a fish from Billingsgate. 'What is all this?' But without her glasses, Mrs Catalyst was unable to read them. Her intention in snatching them from the official was to show him that Mrs Fleggjoy had a champion.

Dickens, having enjoyed his last meal at Periodic Square, spent much of the eventful morning lolling about in the garden at its centre. He noticed the comings and goings as the men in their leather aprons removed the Fleggjoy's goods to the cart, but he seemed to remain indifferent to them.

Soon the moment for the servants' departure arrived. Mary rushed, crying, into the drawing room and then departed quickly. Next, Cook Bleery took her leave of Mrs Fleggjoy: her brother had arrived with his little donkey cart, and she would soon be enjoying the much-deserved comfort of a cup of tea in Camberwell. As a tear or two slipped down her jolly face, she planted a kiss upon her mistress's cheek and then left quickly with a 'God bless you, madam.' But Mrs Fleggjoy was incapable of noticing what was happening and took the sign of affection in the same way that she took the more reserved departures of Jenks and Tetley and, indeed, had taken much of what had happened that day.

It was mid-afternoon when the troubled woman and her housekeeper – who, for reasons that even she could not fathom, was sticking to her mistress – climbed on to the small cart that held the diminished world of the Fleggjoys. The driver with his whip was about to encourage his nag to take off southwards to the river and Southwark when suddenly Mrs Catalyst leapt down from the cart: 'Why bless me, mistress, if we are not forgetting our little chap, Dickens!'

At the very mention of the cat's name, Mrs Fleggjoy seemed to undergo a veritable sea change. 'Dickens?' she said breathlessly. 'Dickens?' That was enough to send them off, scouring the house and the garden for the little fellow.

After much searching, Mrs Catalyst spotted him on a neighbour's wall. 'Dickens!' she shouted. 'Come on, little fellow.' Dickens dutifully climbed down from the wall and leisurely made his way across the neighbouring garden before appearing on the Fleggjoy's garden wall. Then, gingerly dropping down, he was scooped up by Mrs Catalyst as though he had been rescued from a storm-tossed sea. 'Oh, my little fellow, if you only knew how pleased I am to get hold of you.' Tightly locked in the housekeeper's arms, Dickens was taken through the deserted house to join the mistress who, on seeing him, gave him the most committed hug he had ever endured.

They again boarded the patiently waiting cart and were about to leave, only to be witness to the final underlining of the fall of the house of Fleggjoy. A man arrived in a small cart and pulled from the debris of his load a sign which he soon had standing by the railings of the house. It read: 'J. & J.G. Pollyfoot, Estate Agents', and below, in large letters, 'TO BE LET'.

Within the hour, the small, one-ship armada of misfortune was at the gates of the Marshalsea debtors' prison. The sticks of furniture that had been left them were carried through the large, uninviting, high-walled courtyard to their one room. This was to be the home of Mrs Fleggjoy and Mrs Catalyst for as long as the Fleggjoys had no money and no prospect of extricating themselves from their debts – debts, it must be said, that had been forced upon them because Mr Fleggjoy's income over the previous few years was believed to have been 'polluted' by illegal funds.

10

The Bastille

To the troubled, the morrow is oft a long time coming. This particular morrow crept into existence by what seemed the most circuitous of routes, arriving only after a night of tortuous tossing and turning. The two women, unused to sharing a room together, were disturbed by all sorts of perversities of the night, the greatest being that each had a tendency to snore like a bull elephant. Who was the greater or lesser offender would be difficult to judge, but suffice it to say that, when the one was snoring, the other was the audience to this destruction of the night's peace. Dickens himself spent the night trying to get out of the small room. Thus, when the morning did come, he was the first to seek an exit.

The room itself, by the standards of those reduced to a debtors' prison, was adequate. It had, after all, four walls, a floor, a small window and a door. Unlike an ordinary prison, one could come and go through the door as one wished – that is, out into the yard or into the corridors of the Marshalsea. The Fleggjoy room was particularly well sited because it overlooked (though the window hardly afforded a view) the exercise or 'gathering' yard. Here, the inmates and their children and a few servants gathered, played games, talked and hung up washing. And though the place was far from joyful, all the inmates knew that they were lucky not to be in the 'other' place.

Mr Falstaff Fleggjoy was in the 'other' place, in a 'real'

prison, in Newgate, which was the most hated of prisons. In that dungeon, where even the drinking water had to be purchased, Mr Fleggjoy was going through hell on earth. But for the moment, Mr Fleggjoy, out of sight, was out of the minds of the two women and the cat, who got on with living in a space the size of the coal cellar at Periodic Square.

'I'm sorry, my little friend,' said a bleary-eyed Mrs Catalyst to Dickens sitting expectantly at the door. 'You'll 'ave to get used to it, for there is nothing in the world we can do about it.' Getting used to it meant putting up with a soil box in the corner, and a little mat to sleep on, and the alarming constraints of being forced to remain in a room when one had four legs, a good head and a truly marvellous pair of eyes. Two ears of the finest attunement should be added to this list, as well as the appetite not only for eating but also for hunting. And any amount of rolled-up pieces of paper did not compensate for the tantalizing lure of chasing a long tail.

'And don't you go looking at me as though I was a cruel and 'ard-'earted gaoler,' remonstrated the reduced housekeeper.

The thought that Mrs Catalyst might be a gaoler was not a happy one to conjure with, and Mrs Fleggjoy, not yet recovered from the disturbed night she had just spent, gave her a piercing look. 'Don't you mention that word in my presence,' said the look, 'or you'll find yourself looking for another position.' Fortunately the housekeeper was still reflecting on the poor mite Dickens who stood beside the door with all the hopes in the world pinned to his whiskers, and thus Mrs Fleggjoy's bitter thoughts floated away, unfelt by their object. When her mind cleared, Mrs Fleggjoy dwelt on the fact that her housekeeper had stayed with her out of loyalty and not impressment. *Mrs Catalyst*, mused her mistress, *is as free as a bird to go off and seek other employment if she wishes*. So even the troubled Mrs Fleggjoy dared not censure her one remaining and loyal servant.

'You'll just 'ave to make the best of a bad job, my little fellow, for as soon as you got through that door, you would be lost to us for ever.' This further statement addressed to the cat by Mrs Catalyst made a sudden, strong impression on the other woman – that she might lose Dickens to the back streets of Southwark filled her with such pain she picked up the little fellow and squeezed him almost breathless.

Mrs Catalyst went out through the Marshalsea gate and bought a few items that morning for the Fleggjoy larder. A nice fresh loaf of bread was a welcome purchase, and with the few eggs and some bacon she had obtained, there was enough to make a credible breakfast. And as Mrs Catalyst made her purchases, she measured the fortunes of Mrs Fleggjoy against the misfortunes of Mr Fleggjoy who at that moment could be enjoying none of what they were about to enjoy. But then again, mused Mrs Catalyst, he was believed to be a common criminal. A man who had dipped into other people's money was indeed a man not to be pitied. There was, after all, no smoke without fire, and justice must be allowed to take its course.

As Mrs Catalyst returned to the gate of the debtors' prison, it struck her that it was a strange thing indeed to seek voluntary internment in such a place. *Why am I doing this?* she asked herself. *Is it because Mrs Fleggjoy is a good mistress? Is it because 'er cause is worthy and that to support it is the most noble of things? Or is it, and it surely seems more likely, that I have grown sisterly towards the mistress and feel the need to support 'er in 'er hour of need?* Certainly it was not because of a nobility of spirit or a belief in the supremacy of Mrs Fleggjoy over all other mistresses that made her house-keeper stay with her during these troubled times.

For a moment, and possibly for the first time, Mrs Catalyst realized the magnitude of what she was doing. As she stood before the Marshalsea gate, it suddenly dawned on her that it was a sacrifice that few would make and no payment could ever compensate her for it. She was giving up her freedom to live in a boxroom with her mistress and the family pet. She had taken up their fight as though it were her own.

Mrs Catalyst did not hesitate long at the gate. Gathering her thoughts and her shopping, she passed through and resolved at that moment to stay loyal as long as loyalty was called for.

Mrs Fleggjoy, on the return of her housekeeper, looked longingly at the large fresh loaf as though it were a sheaf of gathered sunbeams wrapped in paper that Mrs Catalyst held under her arm. And then the sight of the eggs and the bacon, not to forget a fine piece of country butter, was like a host of saints settling on the table before her. Soon the two women fell to preparing the first meal of the day over the small range that stood in the corner of the small room.

Mistress, housekeeper and family cat busied themselves over the breaking of the night's fast, thankful for the small mercies that they were enjoying, while, a few miles distant, the head of the house of Fleggjoy went through interminable negotiations with his gaoler for the smallest of morsels. As he was a man reduced in fortune, he had not the wherewithal to enjoy even the simplest comforts that a prison could afford – at a price.

At the Marshalsea, Dickens' portion comprised some pieces of fish. He was as pleased as the two women to break his night's fast, but having broken it, he wanted to stretch a leg and scratch an ear in the peace and harmony of the great outdoors. However, once again he was refused an exit and therefore was forced to take refuge under a bed to hide from the fussing of his two companions.

'Oh, my little Dickens,' said Mrs Fleggjoy, 'you just cannot, you just simply cannot.'

And that was the end of it. Dickens was now as caught as any insolvent clerk in the bowels of the law, with no opportunity to do more than pace the floor and sip occasionally from a bowl of tepid water. In short, Dickens, the socially transmogrified cat, was reaping the 'rewards' of mobility.

At luncheon, Mrs Fleggjoy picked at the food that her faithful servant had placed on the table before her. Dickens likewise was similarly indifferent to his victuals. He made a perfunctory sniff at the bowl's contents but his heart was not in it. *Why eat*, his little troubled countenance seemed to say, *when all the world is reduced to a four-walled cell? No long*

tails, no wanderings, no happy jaunts with other cats and the baring of claws and the snarling of snarls. It was enough to turn a cat into a candidate for Bedlam.

Alas, for the moment there was no solution. Soon, perhaps in a matter of weeks, Dickens could be allowed out into the gathering yard for a stroll. By that time, it was to behoped that he would have acclimatized himself to the indifferent room and would have learned how to wander hither and thither without getting lost. But for the moment there was nothing that could be done about the circumstances of the family pet and he would have to get used to that little corner of an English debtors' gaol.

Now that they had survived the morning and were into the afternoon, there seemed a need to do something positive. No further housework was required: the room was already as tidy and neat as two able-bodied women could make it. Mrs Fleggjoy, though, felt it was not enough simply to accept her fate, and she decided to compose a letter to the family solicitor, who needed to be reminded of the dreadful conditions in which they lived and that he should be pressing things forward as quickly as possible.

'Dear Mr Blendthrone,' she began her afternoon missive, 'I think it important that we jolly up things and do what we can to get the matter cleared up as soon as possible. Therefore I would like to know what it is that you is doing to remove my dear husband and meself from this unfortunate position. It is such a <u>dreadful</u> place here, sir, that the very air is enough to drive a body to despair.'

She wrote on for a few pages in this rambling way, which left one as much informed in the end as at the beginning, while Mrs Catalyst got herself ready to take the letter to the offices of Mr Blendthrone, who had the fortune of being retained by the Fleggjoys on all matters legal.

'Mrs Catalyst,' said the mistress once the missive had been carefully placed in the housekeeper's firm grasp, 'you must wait for a reply as it is important that we push this matter

81

forward with the dedication of Zeus.'

'Yes, madam,' said Mrs Catalyst, wondering slightly what Zeus had to do with their situation. And, anyway, it would probably take more than a foreign god to change things for the better. This was only the first day of their incarceration and she had been told by an expert – one of the inmates in the gathering yard – that it took at least three months to get the wheels of the law greased and on the move.

But Mrs Catalyst was game for anything that would take her from the constraints of their new restricted world. Just to walk through Southwark and cross Blackfriars Bridge to Chancery Lane was enough to bring a smile to her face. The only regret she had was that she could not take Dickens with her, for he as much as she needed a bit of time away from the confined space that was now their home.

Once the housekeeper had gone, Mrs Fleggjoy fell to thinking about the possibility that soon they would be out of the mire of the debtors' prison and back on the road to recovery. Once the ridiculous charges against her husband were shown to be false, they could take up from where they had left off. Mrs Fleggjoy then began to think about her house in Periodic Square and all the work that had made it such a splendid place, all the wondrous things that she had put together to create the world in which they had lived so comfortably.

And then the image of the dreadful Mrs Utterpout appeared in her mind with a force that almost knocked her off her stool. 'That woman! That false-'earted woman!' There and then she resolved to close the book on the insults of Periodic Square.

Sitting entirely alone, she could not help but remember the years before Periodic Square as the best of their lives. *Oh, those were the days*, she told herself, *when Mr Fleggjoy and I ...*

Suddenly she realized that she had been so wrapped up in her own problems that she had pushed the thought of that noble man Falstaff Fleggjoy entirely out of her mind. 'Oh, what a woman I am!' she scolded herself. 'To think that I 'ave not given a thought to that man and all his suffering!' She began to weep, overcome by the idea that her husband, who had been branded a common criminal even before he had been tried, was in a far worse state than herself. 'Oh, oh, oh, what a woman I am! What a selfish woman I am!' Racked by tears and moans, she fell upon the bed as she punished herself for not giving the slightest thought to her mewed-up husband.

After a good half an hour of self-scourging she wiped her eyes and sat up on the bed. It was no good doing this to herself, she thought, and looked for Dickens to cheer her up: he would certainly lift her from the doldrums. His delicate face, his long white whiskers, his bright green eyes. Oh, Dickens, Dickens was the life and soul of her happiness!

'Dickens!' she called to the little chap, hoping he would join her on the bed. But no, he did not rush to join her, and Mrs Fleggjoy was reduced to looking for him under the bed. Not finding him there, she had to bend even more uncomfortably to look behind the cupboard.

'Where are you, you little devil?'

Having looked in every conceivable corner of the small room, it finally occurred to her that if Dickens were in that room, he was somewhere that he should not be. But after looking in the oven, she came to the conclusion that he was not there: when Mrs Catalyst had left the room, so had Dickens.

Mrs Fleggjoy again fell on to the bed and let out the worst possible cries of despair. One long scream alerted people in the yard beyond that a woman was in the middle of some dreadful crisis, and that perhaps one or two of them should, out of humanity, knock at the door.

'Are you all right, madam?' came the enquiry after a good few minutes of further painful cries.

To lose one's fortune is one thing. To lose one's respectability is another. But also to lose one's cat when that cat was the only morsel of affection available to a troubled heart is too much to suffer.

When Mrs Catalyst returned late that afternoon, she came with a letter from Mr Blendthrone, which said that everything that could be done was being done, and at this moment there was nothing to be done, only to remember that Mr Fleggjoy in Newgate was having the stickier end of the stick and that Mrs Fleggjoy was living in a relative heaven. This did not endear Mr Blendthrone to Mrs Fleggjoy, but she put all thoughts of recrimination out of her mind. The worst had already happened: Dickens had disappeared and was thus lost to the outside world. She had no idea whether he could survive and prosper. The future had looked bleak before, but now, without Dickens, who had managed to slip the net of the Marshalsea, it looked bleaker still.

Mrs Catalyst and Mrs Fleggjoy faced a second unhappy night aware that somewhere out in the great beyond Dickens was alone.

11

Life Ain't Bad

It is worthy of comment that fecund Nature often casts down a seed to grow in the strangest of places, to prosper where prosperity is not only unlikely but strewn with difficulty. Thus the seed of a great oak might take root in the gutter of a street and flourish there among a trifling amount of mud for half a season. But, we may ask, does wise Nature, great and all-powerful Nature, not know that you cannot drop a seed in a gutter in the city and then expect circumstances to allow it to prosper and bloom there and, in a few hundred years, turn itself into a two-hundred-foot giant?

Is clever Nature not a bit simple if it thinks that the corporation, or the borough, or the municipality, or the parish council will allow a tree to grow at will in the thoroughfare as though it were in the middle of Windsor Great Park or the Savernake Forest?

A stray seedling thus finding sustenance on the hard streets of a city would be unlikely to survive more than a few weeks at the most, among the detritus of man and his animals. Inevitably, along would come a barrow, pushed by some indifferent, Nature-hating mortal who would sweep up the embryo and toss it into his cart and push on up the road. We could hope that the little nascent tree would finally find a resting place on the edge of town where the rubbish of the thoroughfare is dumped. But, alas, we have no guarantee that Nature would not be thwarted again by the crushing and

breaking of its aspirant tree, and that the cycle that Nature desires for all things would not be broken.

Such a preamble, dear reader, has not been written in order to change the protagonist of our story from a cat to an ambitious seedling that aspires to treeness. No, rather it is to underline the sad fact that there is much of Nature's bounty that is lost and broken and thwarted on the city streets, especially in a city as vast as London, where bricks block out the horizon.

But there are other manifestations of Nature that thrive in the city. One of these is, of course, the rat; another is the mouse; another is the sparrow; and still another is the starling. And the chain would not be complete if we did not include the cat. The cat, a gift from the Orient to the West, is the most perfect metropolitan resident, excluding the rodentry. It knows how to make ends meet in the middle, especially when it comes to an empty stomach and a dry throat. And it knows how to harvest the streets as a farmer would harvest his fields.

In spite of what Mrs Fleggjoy might think, Dickens was quite capable of fending for himself on the streets of London. As long as he had those fine eyes and those sharp ears, he would not be defeated in the pursuit of his breakfast or his dinner. The foolish pair who speculated in the cell-room at the Marshalsea would have been better served to reflect on their own precarious prosperity than cause a thought to be directed at the fate of their lovable but not dependent cat.

Dickens had not felt inclined to return to Periodic Square but chose instead to go back to the place of his birth at Dumpling Passage. And sure enough, within a few hours of his escape, he was exactly where he wished to be, a few miles from the Marshalsea on the north side of the river and sitting on a certain wall from the top of which he could survey the whole of the passage.

So, at about the time that Mrs Fleggjoy decided to abandon all hope of a return to Periodic Square, Dickens also set his back on that dreadful place where one might get kicked rather than stroked.

The next day, Dickens was as established as an emperor

surveying his new domain. There was before him all that life required. Food was readily supplied by the presence of the rodentry and the foolish birds that occasionally argued and forgot their place in someone else's food chain. Also, some of the human residents of the passage left out food for other cats, and Dickens was not averse to taking someone else's, if it was left conveniently by a back door. For rest, there was always a quiet place in which to find warmth and cover. It might be in a pile of straw in a deserted house, or occasionally he would permit himself to be taken in and made a fuss of. To be a cat was a joyous state, and the many people who had not one of their own were more than willing to make an arrangement for a passing cat that might be encouraged to stay. And stay Dickens did in some cases. Soon he had as many providers as a handful of cats would require. And in this way did all thoughts of the Fleggjoys disappear with the passing of days, as did the image of the small room filled with the busy presence of two middle-aged women.

It is an indication of the heartless opportunism of cats that Dickens did not bother his head with the fact that his former providers were still confined to small rooms in the bowels of English justice while he cavorted and tortured and slept and drew sustenance from freedom. Dickens, for whom a fortune in Aldeburgh sprats and Aberdeen kippers had been spent, was content to turn to other things and other people.

(Was it not, we may ask ourselves, comparable to prostitution? Was Dickens no better than the hordes of women and children who offered themselves up for a few coins in order to sate the fantasies of men? But, of course, Dickens did not loiter in alleys to participate in the same sorts of economic transactions that passed between twelve-year-old girls and middle-aged bankers. No, there was nothing so crude about Dickens' methods of plying for trade. His means were more subtle than the flaunting of a hip at a cruising gentleman who sought lustful gratification on the way home to a wife who spent her afternoons overseeing charitable efforts and teaching the children little musical vignettes on the piano.

Dickens did not receive money for unnatural acts in this, the third year of the young, virginal Queen's ascendency. He received more tangible things. He received warmth and victuals, while in the streets, girls and boys and women in various states of decay provided services for coins.)

So, in the place of his birth Dickens settled in. And there he would stay.

He was home.

12
Misshapen
Misfortune

'Mrs Catalyst?'

'Yes, madam.'

'Don't you think, my dear, that life is a torture for us?'

'It could be worse, madam.'

'It could, I s'pose.'

'We are in luxury compared with poor Mr Fleggjoy, madam.'

'I s'pose we are.'

This conversation took place one miserable, wet night in the small room at the Marshalsea as Mrs Fleggjoy sat over a game of cards with her housekeeper. The former's despondency seemed more to the fore than usual. 'Poor Mr Fleggjoy. I do miss 'im. Did his situation seem very bad?'

'He looked as though 'e were a man trying to keep 'imself together, madam. I don't know that we 'ave that much to complain about.'

Although this last comment by the housekeeper could be seen as a mild criticism, this was not how it was received by Mrs Fleggjoy. But Mrs Catalyst's journey to carry a small basket of provisions to Newgate the previous day had struck the housekeeper as being similar to a journey into hell – a hell that, by comparison, made of their own place a limbo, simply an uncomfortable waiting room, an anteroom to a real and hateful hell. As she had approached the large, ugly gate of the prison, she had felt her spirits drop like stones to the bottom of a well. And when she had seen Mr Fleggjoy in a crowded alleyway of a room filled with the dirt and disfigurement of the many, he had looked very much a part of the filthy and misshapen rabble. A once-white shirt with a frill at the neck had not distinguished him from the rest; rather, its pitiable state had shown that he was not allowed to pose as a gentleman in that cavernous imprisonment.

'Oh, Mrs Catalyst,' the barely recognizable man sitting on a stool before her had said weakly. 'I do 'ope for pity's sake that you will not suggest to your mistress that I 'ave been reduced to this. It would injure her spirits, I am sure.'

'Yes, sir' had been all the housekeeper could manage to reply as she had stared in ill-disguised horror at this shadow of her mistress's husband.

Then he had fallen upon the pieces of meat and fruit she had brought him, with the indelicacy of a starved dog. As he ate, Mrs Catalyst could only just bring herself to watch: it had been a dread sight. There had been little that she could do or say that would not have immediately revealed her own fallen spirits.

'This is good, Mrs Catalyst, a feast.'

They had sat in the prison room, surrounded by a gaggle of inmates. The dirt had been oppressive; the noise had been the noise of the worst possible type. If she later had the fortune to wander into an art gallery and see the works of Hieronymous Bosch, she might then be able to compare them to an image that she already knew. But in Newgate, she had had nothing to compare that appalling place with, this being her first visit to a *real* prison as opposed to that pleasant domicile called the Marshalsea.

Mr Fleggjoy had continued to ravage the food, but soon, though, his shrunken appetite had brought a heaviness to his stomach and he had been incapable of taking another bite.

'Oh, Mrs Catalyst, if you knew 'ow I appreciated that.'

'Thank you, sir. The mistress was concerned ...'

'But whatever you say,' he had interrupted her, 'you must say nothing of these conditions. Nothing what-so-ever.'

91

The piteous sight of this man whom she had known and worked for had been enough to break her heart. But she had resolved to say nothing, and so she sat there as stone-like as she could. She had also resolved that she would never again complain about the difficulties of her and her mistress's life at the debtors' prison.

Now, as she listened to her mistress complaining about the emptiness of her life, Mrs Catalyst had a strong desire to scream out at her that she was a fool even to think of saying an unhappy word.

The card game was finished. Mrs Fleggjoy packed the cards away and, taking down the great family Bible from its resting place on the window sill, she began to contemplate the travails of the Tribes of Israel, lost in the desert.

Mrs Catalyst in the meanwhile tidied the already tidy room and placed the broom and the dustpan back in the corner. Leaving her mistress to her reflections on the Good Book, she went out into the corridor. There she walked back and forth for a time without much purpose, trying desperately to stop comparing their plenty with the ugliness of the master's state. *Why*, she wondered, *did this fall take place? Why did all of this unhappiness 'ave to be dropped on a 'ead and an 'eart as pure as Mr Fleggjoy's? And why is it that he takes it all so uncomplainingly? Is it*, she surmised, *that the man is truly guilty of the crimes that now 'ave him mewed-up in the dungeons of justice?*

No. She was convinced now in a way she had not been before that Falstaff Fleggjoy was as innocent of the crimes as herself; that, in fact, Mr Fleggjoy was the innocent party in a nest of viperish crooks.

She paced the corridor a little more and then stopped before one of the lamps that threw a little illumination on to the cold flagstones. *If Mr Fleggjoy is not guilty why, then, is he being 'eld? Why, he could die from neglect in such a place!* Suddenly it occurred to her that if Mr Fleggjoy were the innocent party, then someone else must be the guilty one.

'I would wager,' she said out loud, 'that it is that snake-in-the-grass Delloyt.' She continued to pace the floor, totally engrossed in the thought that Mr Fleggjoy could remain in that hell for ever while the real culprit lived on undisturbed.

'Mrs Catalyst?' came a thin, worried voice from the room. Having fulfilled her appetite for the thought that there was no suffering on earth that could not be equalled by biblical suffering, Mrs Fleggjoy was looking for her housekeeper.

'Yes, madam,' came the reply from the dark corridor.

'Oh, Mrs Catalyst, it is so cold out there.' It was cold but the thoughts that rushed through the housekeeper's head had greatly warmed her.

'Do come in, Mrs Catalyst,' pleaded the mistress. 'What is it? Are you not feeling well?'

'I've never felt better, madam,' answered the house-keeper, returning to their room. 'I am just troubled about Mr Fleggjoy and the thought that there lies an innocent man in Newgate and the guilty party is sleeping peacefully in 'is own bed of a night.'

Mrs Catalyst had never spoken to her mistress like this before, and Mrs Fleggjoy was slightly taken aback. 'But Mrs Catalyst,' she said, though really she had nothing to say.

Mrs Catalyst now began pacing the floor of the small room. There was a questing as well as a firmness to her step, as though in the pacing she was beginning to put together something in her head, something like a citadel of good sense, as if she had found a way out once and for all, of their needless waiting and the Fleggjoy's joint incarceration. What were they waiting *for*? For justice to be done? Why, injustice existed at that very moment in the desperate figure of that gentleman, Mr Fleggjoy. Could justice grow or develop out of the blindness of injustice? If nothing were done, her mind ran, would not it be possible that they would all remain in their respective into-lerable circumstances until the Day of Judgement?

As she paced back and forth, she pounded her left palm with her right fist. These actions of the big, strong and forceful Mrs Catalyst rather overwhelmed Mrs Fleggjoy, and caused her to reflect that perhaps her housekeeper, now without a house to tend, was slipping into a kind of dementia.

'We must push Mr Blendthrone, madam. 'e must be pushed to do something for Mr Fleggjoy rotting up there at Newgate.'

'Rotting? *Rotting?*' Mrs Fleggjoy was stunned by the graphic term.

Mrs Catalyst now turned and, looking angrily, bitterly and with a certain aggression said, 'Mrs Fleggjoy, as sure as the sun rises in the morning and as sure as it sets in the evening, Mr Fleggjoy will die if we don't push things on.'

Mrs Fleggjoy slumped on to the bed. The very hard and committed words of her servant had taken her breath away. *It is a cruel blow*, she may have thought, *to be delivered when life is so difficult for me*. But the blow had been delivered with such conviction that Mrs Fleggjoy seemed persuaded of its truth.

They spent the last hours of that day, and a few into the night, composing another letter to Mr Blendthrone. Unlike the last, it was full of pointed and bitter observations, its purpose being to get Mr Plowload Blendthrone off his well-upholstered backside and out of his well-upholstered office so that he would get about the business of justice. This letter, which Mrs Catalyst would deliver to the Chancery Lane the following morning, would be a battering ram against Mr Blendthrone's lackadaisical performance in securing the release of Mr Falstaff Fleggjoy from the gutters of hell.

'And of course, you know,' said an animated Mrs Fleggjoy as she prepared for bed in the early hours, 'that my dear husband was instrumental in making Mr Blendthrone into the prosperous man he is today. Why, he had nothing before Mr Fleggjoy gave 'im custom and contacts. Nothing.'

Now was the time to remind him of that fact, and to exact some favours.

Although both women were restless for a short while, they soon fell into a refreshing sleep, their just reward for taking positive action. And for the first time since his disappearance, neither woman wondered where Dickens was.

And on the morrow, the wheels of justice would have to start turning – or else!

13

Actions
Speak Loudest

We must, for the moment, continue to forget our furry friend and watch again the rising of the two women in their small cell in the Marshalsea. There was a new spring in Mrs Catalyst's step and a desire to press on. Dressed, ablutions complete and a light sustenance taken, she wrapped herself in her shawl and, taking leave of her mistress, stepped out through the Marshalsea gate and made her way towards Blackfriars Bridge. As she went, Mrs Catalyst ignored the comings and goings of London's commerce, nor did she comment, as numerous commentators had, on the imbroglio of the streets. What did she care for the rushing porters and the carriers and the draymen and the carriages that plied their trade on the streets of London?

Of course, it was the letter and its contents that activated Mrs Catalyst into rushing, headlong and oblivious, through the London byways. All she wished to do, and she pictured herself doing it, was forcibly ram the letter into the hands of Mr Plowload Blendthrone and demand that, irrespective of other commitments, he would sort out the Fleggjoy's problems there and then.

Mrs Catalyst, committed and determined, was soon striding down New Bridge Street and up Fleet Street (only a stone's throw, should she have had time to look, from Dickens' new hunting grounds), towards the offices of Blendthrone, Buludily & Heatherdeckle in Chancery Lane. 'I'll get that man moving,' Mrs Catalyst told herself as she strode on with the

determination of Hannibal crossing the Alps, 'or I'll *explode* in the attempt.'

Mrs Catalyst, of course, did not for one moment say to herself that it was not her place to fight for her master's survival, that it should have been Mrs Fleggjoy moving heaven and earth to rescue him from certain death. No, Mrs Catalyst took it upon herself in the best spirit of the British, who had always contrived for the lower classes to fight the battles of the upper. So it should be and so it was.

Passing now the wedding-cake spire of St Bride's, her resolve was not in the slightest diminished by the walk, though a fair sweat was upon her brow. She pushed forward to Chancery Lane and the offices of the indifferent and lackadaisical MrBlendthrone. It was not long before Mrs Catalyst was climbing the steps that led to the offices of the family solicitor. On reaching the top, she came upon a bulky individual in the process of descending and was forced to flatten herself against the wall to allow him to pass.

'Thank you, madam' came the courteous reply from the large personage, and as he came level with the perspiring housekeeper, he tried the difficult manoeuvre of removing his hat to show his respect for both her sex and her flattening. It was only then that Mrs Catalyst noticed that the bulk belonged to none other than Mr Plowload Blendthrone himself, senior partner and legal representative of the Fleggjoy family.

'Mr Blendthrone?' Mrs Catalyst enquired.

'I have that pleasure,' replied the man.

'I am Mrs Fleggjoy's 'ousekeeper,' Mrs Catalyst barked back, conscious of the need to take up the cudgels then and there, to frighten the man and not allow him to run away to a so-called important meeting that would probably keep him out of the office for the rest of the day, if not for the week.

'Oh, really? . . . ' Mr Blendthrone said and, in the hope of enlarging on this, left his mouth hanging open. Alas, he was not permitted and he was thus stuck, open-mouthed and belly-to-belly, against the flattened Mrs Catalyst on the narrow stairway.

'Now, Mr Blendthrone,' Mrs Catalyst began her half-rehearsed assault, 'I do not want no excuses or words or whatever. I want action, else that man, that simple and foolish man, will die up there at the Newgate before they find out that it was not 'im that did them things, but that it was that man, *Mister* Delloyt, 'ho was the only one 'ho could 'ave done them things.'

As she paused to catch her breath, Mr Blendthrone let out a soft, supplicating 'Yes'. Then Mrs Catalyst took up her verbal cudgels again, this time about the iniquities of Mr Falstaff Fleggjoy's imprisonment.

'... And if you was to ask my opinion, sir, though I was not there and only came to their employ after, Mr Delloyt took Mr Fleggjoy as party in order to cover up and rob and thieve and set Mr Fleggjoy up as the man who in the end would take the blame. For there is not a man who looks at the world so softly and so unaware as Mr Fleggjoy. Though he can be right tough on certain things, he did truly kneel at the feet of that Delloyt, all the while Delloyt was robbing, making it look as though it were that foolish man who, for his softness, now lays up there at Newgate, rotting like a badly kept cauliflower. I tell you, sir, if you do not get your wits about you, he'll becarried out in a shroud soon enough. And if I might finish on this point: you owe much to this man 'cause it was 'im that first gave you business and encouraged you to the 'eights you now are on.'

Mrs Catalyst said all this with such conviction and such aggression that it would have frightened the wind out of the sails of the toughest of legal avoiders. But apart from taking a theatrical extra deep breath at the suggestion that he owed all to Fleggjoy's patronage (a difficult thing for the best of men to accept), Blendthrone listened with what could only be described as great intensity – and in spite of the fact that the listener and the narrator were pressed incommodiously together on the stairs.

A silence fell between them once Mrs Catalyst had exhausted her stream of information, liberally seasoned with invective. It was only broken when Mr Blendthrone turned with great awkwardness and started to walk back upstairs.

'If you will accompany me,' said the corpulent legal brain.

'Why yes, sir' came the reply of the woman who had expected a barrage of excuses rather than a request to enter the inner sanctum. Once through the office door, Mr Blendthrone ushered Mrs Catalyst into his private office and, closing the door behind him, begged her to take a seat.

'Mrs ...?'

'Catalyst.'

'Ah yes, Catalyst. A fine name. Yes, well, Mrs Catalyst, you have arrived at just the right moment. In fact, you may have saved me a visit this very afternoon to the Marshalsea. In short, I have some very interesting news for your mistress.'

Mrs Catalyst was not entirely convinced that this was not part of the whirligig of legal words within which legal brains hide themselves in pursuance of their desire to be elsewhere. For the moment she accepted the spirit of what the man said but, sitting attentively in her chair, waited for him to continue with 'I shall act expeditiously, at some not too distant time in the future.'

However, Mr Blendthrone picked up from his desk a letter addressed to Mrs Fleggjoy at the Marshalsea, handed it to Mrs Catalyst and smiled. 'Here, my good woman, is the letter which explains all with reference to the Fleggjoy situation. I think you will not find it unworthy or uninteresting. But as you have so kindly come all this way, and presumably by foot –'

'By foot,' she agreed.

'Yes, by foot ... therefore I think it is incumbent on me to explain to you the nature of what you now have in your hands. The letter explains that the Fleggjoy internment is about to draw to a rapid close. A close that is occurring far earlier than I had hitherto believed possible, simply on the basis that the law in my experience, in order to be efficient, has to move grindingly slow ...'

But Mrs Catalyst was not listening to the little

embellishments that Mr Blendthrone gave to his speech. It was typical, Mrs Catalyst mused, for a legal person to make a simple thing sound complex in order that he might charge more for his time.

'Does this mean, sir,' Mrs Catalyst interrupted curtly after the man had embellished so much that she feared that he had completely forgotten the urgent matter before them, 'does this mean that Mr Fleggjoy will be freed from the Newgate?' She asked this with a twist of her mouth that exposed her inner feeling.

Mr Blendthrone, being a man who had not got to his present position of prominence without learning to read the thoughts of others, immediately curtailed his verbal romp and came straight to the point: 'On the morrow, on the very morrow.'

'Are you saying, sir ...' she repeated hesitatingly, unbelievingly, 'that Mr Fleggjoy is leaving the Newgate prison *tomorrow?*'

'There is no question about it. The documents are to be signed this very afternoon. I was on my very way this very moment to the very judge in chambers.'

Mrs Catalyst was stunned. The image that had been haunting her – of an innocent man dying at Newgate while the world fumbled with legalities – immediately disappeared. She smiled.

Mr Blendthrone rang a small bell and, between the first and last ring, the door was opened and a supplicant member of the tribe of obsequious legal clerks entered.

'Mr Grosgroull, would you kindly bring Mrs Catalyst some refreshment?'

'Certainly, sir,' said the clerk as he bent solicitously over his master, 'and what will it be, madam? A cordial? A coffee? A tea? Or perhaps a drop of early morning sherry?' It was indeed early to be offered such a range, and it must be said that, in polite society, the last item would not have been included. But then Mr Blendthrone and his clerk and his whole establishment in Chancery Lane were of quite new social coinage.

For the first time, Mrs Catalyst was flustered by the

attention now proffered by a man who knew the advantage of a hard voice and an aggressive tone. Having expected to battle her way through, she was not prepared for his retreat and open surrender.

'Well, er, er,' she fumbled. 'P'haps a, er, yes, a cordial.'

The man took himself off to fetch the requested drink, and Mr Blendthrone now turned again to the subject that concerned them both.

'As you are aware, Mrs Catalyst,' he began, 'Mr Fleggjoy was solely blamed for embezzling the accounts and abusing the trust of the clients of the busines of which he was a partner?'

'Yes, sir.'

'Now, much of this was based on the word of the senior partner, Mr Delloyt. It was he who, when the complaints were laid at the company's feet, directed suspicion at Mr Fleggjoy. The complaints came from two clerks who noted the discrepancies and knew them to be coming from the higher reaches of the company. These two clerks brought the matter to the attention of the authorities, and Mr Delloyt then accused his lesser partner. Thus it was Mr Fleggjoy who was imprisoned, not because he had been found guilty but because it was believed he might make a dash. And, as you know, his monies were frozen because it was believed that much of them came from his alleged nefarious deals.'

Mrs Catalyst sat rigid in the chair and did not even notice when Mr Blendthrone's clerk crept back into the office with the cordial and placed it before her on the desk. He left, also without being noticed, but he was, we can rest assured, used to this and made nothing of it.

'So you might say that Mr Delloyt was the chief prosecution witness, and let me emphasize, my good woman, his social standing meant he would be believed before he had even opened his mouth. But as the days grew fewer between the accusation and the trial, Mr Delloyt realized that it might not be possible to keep up the pretence. That is what I believe, for why else would he attempt to skip off to the Continent?'

'Skip off, sir?' asked Mrs Catalyst with a certain alarm in

103

her voice.

'Oh no, do not worry yourself – he did not manage to do so.'

Mrs Catalyst breathed a sigh of relief and, noticing the cordial for the first time, sipped a refreshing mouthful.

'Do carry on, sir,' commanded the housekeeper as though she were listening to the most riveting of fictitious tales.

'Well, he did try his best to get himself on the Dover packet to Calais. He got to the port of his departure without incident, but, alas for him, in the process of boarding the packet he was knocked down and fatally injured by the very vehicle that had conveyed him thus far. Fortunately for our business, I had an agent following this duplicitous man, who was therefore witness to the accident. He allowed Delloyt, as the life ebbed out of him, the chance to make a clean breast of things, and this final confession was also witnessed no less than by a Justice of the Peace, likewise on his way to France but for more Christian reasons than the by then fast-fading Delloyt. The latter's confession enabled him, we can only hope, to face the gates of the hereafter with equanimity.'

Mr Blendthrone, who loved to tell a story, as long as it reflected on his perspicacity and legal supremacy, now chuckled, his large frame puffed up like that of a bantam cock, as he awaited the declarations of admiration from the overawed housekeeper. It was largely in anticipation of the joy of being told how clever he was that he had allowed her to enter his office and partake of his refreshments.

However, he was to be disappointed. 'Is all you 'ave told me in the letter to my mistress?' was Mrs Catalyst's only response to his thrilling rendition.

'More or less. And let me add that soon, very soon indeed, all the assets of the Fleggjoys' will be unfrozen. Though your ·employers may not be as "comfortable" as they once were, due to the debts of the company of which Mr Fleggjoy is now the only functioning partner, a decent living will be salvaged, I am sure.'

Mrs Catalyst sat lost in thought. Mr Blendthrone twitched

impatiently, somewhat irritated that there had been no mention of his towering performance.

'So what will 'appen?' asked Mrs Catalyst after what seemed to the lawyer an interminable and undemonstrative silence.

' "Happen", ma'am?' repeated the now slightly deflated legal charmer. 'Why, Mr Fleggjoy will be joining you at the Marshalsea some time tomorrow morning. Then I should think that within a matter of days we shall see a leaving of that place to more salubrious accommodations. In short, my good woman, the Fleggjoys' sojourn in hell is over.'

The Fleggjoy housekeeper stood without more ado, tucked the solicitor's letter securely in her bosom and left the office. If she had looked over her shoulder, she would have seen Mr Blendthrone's glare. Luckily, she had not devised the art of mind reading, which, in the case of Mr Plowload Blendthrone, would have been an ugly experience.

Out in the street, Mrs Catalyst drew a deep breath of the warm summer air and exaltedly turned and walked back the way she had come. Although she was not as vigorous in her going as she had been in her coming, none the less she was soon approaching the river that divided the world of London.

14
Relief

In the interests of privacy, the complete details of the arrival of Mr Fleggjoy at the Marshalsea will not be related. That the poor man did arrive and was hugged by his wife and even embraced by his housekeeper is enough to show that he was given a genuine welcome in their reduced circumstances. But when he enquired, 'what in 'eaven's name has happened to Dickens?' he was given a disappointing answer.

' 'e did, sir,' said Mrs Fleggjoy, 'move with us, but he did not 'onour us with his presence for long. I should say it was no more than a day before he was off to other parts, parts that were not so cramped, no doubt. And we 'ave seen no more of him, and I would therefore like to finish with this subject here and now and not 'ave it mentioned again.'

Mr Fleggjoy, of course, protested, greatly concerned with finding out where the little fellow actually was. Had they not sought him out? Had they not scoured the gardens at Periodic Square? Had they not done anything? But Mr Fleggjoy's questions only resulted in a sharp exchange.

'I shall not be answerable, Falstaff Fleggjoy, as to why I did not 'ave my only member of staff searching the streets. Enough is enough.'

And that was the end of the subject. They said no more. Mr Fleggjoy, who felt not his old robust self, ceased his queries about whether they had looked for the cat or where the cat could be at that moment. He realized that the strains of the

reduced Fleggjoy situation might cause the matter to blow up into something bigger than it really was.

But Fleggjoy loved his cat. He missed him and had been looking forward to seeing him and stroking his sleek black fur. But no, he had gone and was probably by now part of a cheap fur coat at Whitechapel.

Mr and Mrs Fleggjoy and Mrs Catalyst sat down to a meal that should have been joyous, but the fate of Dickens hung like a black cloud over the whole of the repast. As they ate, they tried to be jolly and smile at each other, but the spectre of the lost little fellow left a nasty taste in at least Mr Fleggjoy's mouth.

You can imagine that if the circumstances of the two women at the Marshalsea had been difficult, then the arrival of Mr Fleggjoy into their midst caused even a greater strain. But he was wise enough that afternoon to wander out into the gathering yard and do what the two women had failed to do: he introduced himself and chatted and soon you could hear in the room the echoing sounds of Mr Fleggjoy's loud laugh and voice and those of his companions. But when he came in with a merry face Mrs Fleggjoy gave him a look that suggested that he had overstepped the mark.

The first night was murderous. At five of the clock, as dawn approached, so bad had the circumstances become that Mr Fleggjoy went out and walked about the yard. *'ow long can we endure such conditions?* he mused. *Is it possible that we might also 'ave another room in which Mrs Fleggjoy and I can 'ave some privacy?*

After breakfast, a heavily breathing Mr Plowload Blendthrone came calling, entirely unannounced. To reinforce his obvious social superiority (obvious to Mr Blendthrone, that is), he pulled out a large spotted handkerchief and dusted down the seat that Mrs Fleggjoy offered to him.

'Ah, madam, sir, Mrs Catalyst,' he said with a sigh as he lowered his bulk on to the new dust-free seat. 'How pleased I am to see that you are surviving. But I have for you the good news that you have been waiting for. I have arranged that, in two days' time, your incarceration will indeed be over. You will be leaving this place once and for all, and will, one hopes, be on the road to reconstruction.'

This news was greeted with the slapping of backs and the banging together of hands. It was also accompanied by a few kisses distributed between housekeeper, mistress and master. In fact, only the fat man was excluded from the congratulations, an exclusion that slightly hurt his *amour propre* as, after all, it had been he who had engineered the happy event. Mr Fleggjoy, however, did slightly compensate for the solicitor's hurt feelings by proffering a soft hand to be shaken vigorously by the seated, perspiring and fat legal expert.

'You will forgive me, madam, sir, if I immediately acquaint you with a less happy fact. Although most of your assets will be released to you, they will be greatly reduced, and the very pride of your prosperity, No. 17 Periodic Square, will still have to be sold to pay off the debts of the brokerage partnership.' As Mr Blendthrone said this, he had the air of one who had been saving bad news to follow good. But to his surprise, neither Mrs Fleggjoy nor her partner nor their housekeeper made the smallest of protests.

'Well, if it must be, sir, it must, I'm sure, be,' said Mr Fleggjoy.

'Surely you know the situation best, sir,' added his wife.

'I could have, of course, saved the house, but the expense of maintaining it would have been too, too much for your more straitened circumstances, sir, madam. So I thought that it was better to lose the house and preserve your income, sir, madam, though even that will be reduced.'

His comments brought not a drop of dissension, and to the legal brain's surprise he was allowed to complete his peroration without the suggestion of it arising.

'But now we must get on to the question of where you will remove to on the morrow's morrow. That I feel is still a problem. And therefore the only thing I can suggest is your removal to Dumpling Manor – for, as you know, this is the only property that you own at this moment – until such time

109

that you can set yourselves up properly. Then we can survey the scene for something more appropriate for a reduced but still respectable Fleggjoy household.'

'But did you say "Dumpling Manor"?' asked Mrs Fleggjoy with a look of incredulity.

'I did, madam,' replied Mr Blendthrone. 'But I must say, before we debate this matter the more, that under the present circumstances there is very little choice for you to go elsewhere.'

A strange look crossed Mrs Fleggjoy's face, as if she had heard something that was far from believable.

'But what is "Dumpling Manor", if I might ask?' she queried.

Mr Fleggjoy and Mr Blendthrone looked at each other.

A moment's silence ensued and then Mr Fleggjoy cleared his throat and explained. 'Why, Mrs Fleggjoy, I might 'ave at some stage overlooked to tell you of an odd purchase I made shortly after we moved to Periodic Square. The purchase was, my dear, the 'ouse at Dumpling Passage that we had been no more than renters of. And in the process, I 'ad it improved, not grandly, mind, and now it is renamed "Dumpling Manor".' He said this in an as matter-of-fact way as he could, not wishing his wife to think that he had indeed been capable of doing anything underhand. But Mrs Fleggjoy was not capable in the least of thinking the worst of Mr Fleggjoy. All she could manage to do was walk over and kiss her husband.

Shortly afterwards, Mr Blendthrone left the Marshalsea Prison, aware that he had not only performed a great duty but that this had been accepted as though it had been the least he could do.

The Fleggjoy household spent the next day packing and preparing for the moment when they would be free of the labyrinths of justice. Thus, with their thoughts on the future, they bore the cramped conditions of those last two nights with equanimity.

15

Dumpling Manor

You will have noticed that the leitmotif of our story dodged out of sight for more than a few pages. Dickens, while good fortune was being revived in that place of incarceration south of the river, had got used to the idea that he was now entirely on his own. The fact was, of course, that Dickens was not all alone. He had simply got used to new conditions, and these conditions were that, although he was no longer beholden to one, he soon became beholden to the many. Now he was recognized as an adjunct of Dumpling Passage, ever ready to skin a long tail or take a morsel or two from the mouths of other cats. He graced the place as a 'character', a loner, a wanderer, one who was prepared to do what he felt like with a complete lack of feeling. One night he might rest in the kitchen of an old woman, another in the loft of a decayed inebriate. Whatever he decided to do, he did according to his own lights, and he was as unpredictable as the clouds that lowered over the small locale of his nativity. Dickens thus was not a tied beast. He did and came as he wanted to do and come, and he was loved for it. And there were many who were prepared to do as he wished – that is, lay out a plate for him or do his bidding by leaving a window open.

One special morning, a large waggon arrived at the house in which he had once lived as a kitten. The unloaders he may have recognized, but Dickens himself remained out of sight, watching. Soon the unloading was complete and, with it,

the house, now nicely retitled 'Dumpling Manor'.

The Fleggjoys fell in love with their new assured freedom. They were not wealthy, but from now on, with moderation, they would always be comfortable. Mrs Catalyst, their loyal retainer, decided to stay where she was. She would housekeep. And Mr Fleggjoy would learn the art of going to the market and buying vegetables and fruit and doing what was expected of him. His library of self-improving novels was his greatest asset. And he was happy.

One day, on catching sight of Dickens, he let out a yelp of recognition and was almost ready to embrace him. But no, at that moment Mrs Fleggjoy came out.

'Mr Fleggjoy! Mr Fleggjoy!' she screeched. 'As long as I 'ave breath in my body, that cat will not be taken into this 'ouse or given any sustenance. For did he not in our grimmest hour desert us? Did he not unceremoniously shuffle off to do what he wished and cared not a jot for our suffering? I tell you, sir, I would not want that animal in my 'ouse if 'e was the last animal in the world, and that is the last of it!'

Her anathematizing of the cat was the final rupture between Dickens and the house of Fleggjoy. And there was nothing that Mr Fleggjoy or Mrs Catalyst could do about it, except leave out for him the odd piece of food.

The Fleggjoys settled in. On occasions that filled them with a sense of irony, they could be found walking up to Periodic Square to look at their former home. They enjoyed the thought that, though they were now more humble, they were no longer bloated and foolish. Often they would see the cat that no longer existed, sitting in the jungle in the middle of the square and imagining what he wished. At other times, the Fleggjoys were to be found enjoying the Good Book together. It filled them with the hope of eternal life.

Once, when the Fleggjoys were taking the air at Periodic Square, they saw a fat woman struggling towards No. 17. She stopped and knocked. She smiled at the maid. She was ushered in.

The Fleggjoys had seen the promised land, built on promissory notes, and they liked none of it.

Dickens grew ignorant of his early travails. And with this, he became a slower and gentler fellow.

finis